To all those men and women who have served in our military in times of war and peace. This includes my father, Bruce A. Dobbs, who served in World War II aboard the USS Salt Lake City in the Pacific Theater; and my father-in-law, Stanley J. Widziewicz, who served in the US Army in the latter days of World War II while preparing for the invasion of Japan.

www.mascotbooks.com

Sacrifice at Shenandoah

For more information, please contact:
Mascot Books
560 Herndon Parkway #120
Herndon, VA 20170
info@mascotbooks.com

Library of Congress Control Number: 2015915524

CPSIA Code: PBANG1115A
ISBN-13: 978-1-63177-229-0

Printed in the United States

Sacrifice at Shenandoah

by Gerry Dobbs

Prologue

Late that afternoon, two blue-clad soldiers rode their mounts toward a heavily wooded section of the Blue Ridge Mountains, following the scanty trail of the men they were tracking. The older of the two, a sergeant, had a chin covered with black and silver whiskers and deeply set eyes hooded by black, bushy eyebrows. The younger was a private with medium-brown mustache and sideburns and a confident quality about him that men found comforting and easy to follow.

As they entered a hemlock hollow fed by a small stream, they dismounted to water their horses. Something caught the sergeant's eye. He quietly tapped the young private on the shoulder and pointed toward a plume of smoke coming from a cave several yards up the mountain. The sergeant motioned for the young private to follow him through the undergrowth toward the cave, signaling stop when he heard voices inside the cave.

After a few minutes listening intently, the sergeant turned and motioned with his head to return to their horses. The private reached his horse first and took out a pencil and notebook from his saddlebag, then quickly scribbled a message. He nodded his head with satisfaction, then ripped the page from his notebook. He folded it neatly into a small rectangle and swiftly tucked it away.

The silence near the creek was shattered when a gunshot whizzed by them coming from the direction of the cave. Instinctively, the two men skirted behind their horses, reaching for their weapons. Just as the sergeant was loading his Navy Colt pistol, another shot rang out. The young private heard the all too familiar, sickening thud, then a soft groan.

The sergeant slowly crumpled to his knees, blood oozing from his right shoulder. As he reached to put pressure on the wound, another shot grazed the left side of his head. More shots rained down into the hollow. The private quickly helped the dazed sergeant onto his horse. The sergeant gave instructions to hold steady while he went to bring reinforcements from camp.

While the sergeant spoke, the young private slipped a small brown package into the sergeant's saddlebag. Then the private smacked the horse's rump, sending it galloping toward the east.

Not knowing when help would arrive, the private turned back to the source of the gunshots. Facing unknown enemies, he took his Sharps breech-loading rifle and knelt behind a tree. He closed his eyes and muttered what seemed to be a prayer, then took the cartridge box from his shoulder. He opened its flap and placed it on the ground, allowing easy access to more cartridges.

Methodically, the private loaded his rifle, using the scope to search for adversaries on the ridge. With his well-honed sharp-shooting skills, he fired on the ridge, hitting a man in the leg, seemingly determined to only wound with his shots. Soon more men appeared at the mouth of the cave, including a Union officer.

As the gun fire increased, a shot came from his left flank catching him by surprise and tearing into his left hand. He dropped his rifle, clutching his hand in pain.

Realizing he was now surrounded, he looked up into the blue sky and reverently commended himself to the Father. With renewed strength and grit, he stood and picked up his rifle and with careful aim, wounded two more men.

Another shot rang out, hitting him squarely in the chest and exiting his back. The bullet's impact violently forced him to spin around, falling to the ground. Clenching his teeth and grimacing in severe pain, the young private reached inside his jacket and with a shaking hand pulled out a small leather pouch.

As he propped himself on his elbow, another shot smacked dead center into his back. This time, the bullet's violent impact forced him facedown toward the creek where he softly whispered his last word, "Mary!"

Chapter One

"Boy, it's hot!" grumped Stephen.

The summer had been dragging on and on without any sign of relief from the unrelenting heat. After enduring several dog days of summer, Stephen plopped down on the couch next to Cassie and said, "We need to get away for from this heat. It's just plain miserable!"

Cassie smiled and suggested, "Let's take off some time from work next week and go to Shenandoah National Park. It's been ages since we camped up there - not since JD was little. And remember how nice it was in the evenings during our honeymoon?"

"I really like that idea! It would be nice to camp up in the mountains again. Tell you what, Cassie - when we go, I promise we'll spend the last night in an air-conditioned motel complete with a hot shower!"

Cassie and Stephen grinned at each other, remembering their honeymoon camping trip over 30 years earlier.

On Saturday, they enthusiastically packed their camping gear into the car. Soon, they were traveling toward the Blue Ridge Mountains, their memories drifting easily to when they first met as students at Virginia Tech. The timeless mountains seemed welcoming, promising them that the journey from their hectic life in the D.C. suburbs would be rewarded with a cool, relaxing week. It was easy for them to lapse into the old folk tune,

Shenandoah, the closer they got to the mist-covered mountains.

By late afternoon, they were at the southern end of Shenandoah National Park. A few miles later, they arrived at Loft Mountain campground. They chose a campsite with a large tree canopy overhead and set about pitching the tent. After laying their bedding on the tent floor, Stephen began to gather wood to start a fire. Although most of the dry kindling had already been gathered by other campers, he found enough sticks to start a nice campfire. Cassie searched through the ice chest and food bin for the items she needed to cook dinner.

Soon, the crackling red hot embers were ideal for roasting hot dogs. They relaxed while eating, quenching their thirst with cool iced tea. Stephen sighed contentedly, "There's nothing like a cold drink from an ice-filled cooler!"

As the sun settled behind the mountains, the night breezes pulled cooler air around them. Cassie yawned, "It's been a long day - I'm ready to hit the sack. Will you put out the fire?"

Down to just glowing embers, Stephen carefully stirred their dinner dishwater into the fire until it was safely out, then joined Cassie in their tent for a good night's sleep.

Cuddled in their double-wide sleeping bag with Cassie's head on his shoulder, Stephen listened to the night breezes rustling the leaves in the treetops above the tent. The air temperature soon dropped to a comfortable, cool level they hadn't felt for quite some time. It wasn't long before the lulling effect of the mountains had done its persuasive work in putting the couple to sleep.

Chapter Two

Stephen awoke to the sound of birds chirping overhead. Enjoying the cool morning, he started a campfire while Cassie finished dressing in their tent. Soon they sat down to a wonderful breakfast of coffee, scrambled eggs, and bacon. As they ate, Stephen and Cassie made plans to hike a portion of the Appalachian Trail toward the Ivy Creek shelter. After washing their dishes, putting away food, and dousing the fire, they prepared for a hike to Ivy Creek.

Starting down the trail, their senses became fully engaged. Once again, they were enamored with the extraordinary beauty of Shenandoah National Park. The grassy opening of the campground gave way to a cool canopy from the hardwoods lining both sides of the trail. As they meandered down the trail, Stephen and Cassie took spurs that led to amazing views. One in particular ended at a rocky overlook where they watched hawks soaring effortlessly on the wind currents high above the dark-green tree canopy below.

Eventually they came to the Ivy Creek shelter where the spring water flowed effortlessly from a pipe peeking out from the sloping hillside. The water was cool, clear, and quite refreshing. They rinsed their hands and filled their water bottles. The shelter and spring were so welcoming they found it difficult to leave to continue their hike down the trail.

Before long, Stephen and Cassie came across what they

thought was a spur even though it wasn't marked as part of the Ivy Creek trail. Wanting to explore, they took the unmarked trail.

As they continued further down the path, the canopy of the trees became so dense it allowed very little light through to the ground. There was a steep slope on one side of the path, dropping several yards to a dark hollow filled with immense hemlocks and mountain laurel.

Walking single file down the narrow path, Stephen felt Cassie tap him on the shoulder. Pointing beyond him, she whispered, "Deer!" They froze in place to watch deer grazing in the small clearing ahead.

Trying to get closer, Stephen stepped forward, his eyes fixed on the deer. Moving his left foot forward, he stepped down on what he thought was solid ground. The edge of the narrow path gave way, and Stephen found himself tumbling down the steep slope over rocks and roots to the dark hollow below. Fortunately, he landed on a layer of soft, cushiony hemlock needles deposited on the forest floor over many decades.

Cassie anxiously called, "Are you all right?"

After checking himself for any serious injuries, he answered, "Yep! I feel kinda foolish, but I'm okay."

"Stay put! I'm coming down," she replied.

As Cassie found a way to safely get down to where he was, Stephen stood and brushed off the debris from his pants and shirt. His eyes soon became accustomed to the dim light. Scanning the surrounding landscape, he noticed a small creek running through the hollow. It was easy to see that the creek typically flowed to a width of 6 to 8 feet, but the recent drought had reduced it to a 12-inch trickle.

He walked to the creek and waited there while Cassie carefully picked her way down to him. As Stephen scanned the other bank of the creek, something caught his eye, begging him to investigate.

Hopping to the opposite creek bank, he walked over and picked up the object—an old canteen. The sling normally attached to the canteen was rotted away, and it looked like it probably had come with a stopper instead of the usual screw-on cap.

As he stood there wondering how old the canteen actually was, Cassie caught up to him. "Are you sure you're okay, Stephen? What's that?"

"Looks like an old canteen," Stephen replied.

She shrugged, "It was probably left behind by some hiker."

"I'm not sure about that - it looks antique, but who knows... you're probably right, Cassie."

As Stephen stooped to put it back on the ground, Cassie stepped backward out of his way. Catching her heel on something hard, she landed with a thud. He chuckled ready to tease her about having a nice trip until he saw the startled look on her face and said, "What's wrong, Cassie? Are you hurt?"

"Stephen, look—I think it's a pipe of some sort." She moved to reveal what looked like a long, metal pipe. Stephen knelt down and started brushing away the old hemlock needles and other debris from around the pipe-like object. "It's not a pipe, Cassie. It looks like a rifle barrel!"

He continued to brush away the organic debris, uncovering the wooden end of the rifle. Stephen saw markings on the rifle butt, and said to Cassie, "I can't quite make out what it says. Let me try this..." He proceeded to rub a handful of the composted hemlock needles into the markings on the rifle butt. As Stephen rubbed, the markings became darker. "Look! They're initials - E. L. D. Hmmm... there's something else above the initials. Looks like a caliper over a builder's square -- a Masonic symbol."

Cassie looked at him, "What are you thinking? This sure isn't something you'd typically find on the Appalachian Trail."

"This rifle and canteen look like they belong to the Civil

War time period. I wonder..." He paused, gazing around.

"What?" prompted Cassie.

"I wonder if there are more Civil War artifacts here. I'd like to look some more to see if we can find anything else."

Cassie looked at the sky, "Okay, but we don't have much time. It looks like the sun will be setting soon."

They started moving away from each other, eyes to the ground. Within a few minutes, Cassie's gaze caught the late afternoon sun glinting off something on the ground. She reached down to pick up the shiny object. Her eyes widened with excitement as she gazed at it. "Stephen, check this out!"

She handed Stephen a button with two flags crossing over each other and a torch behind them. "What do you think?" asked Cassie.

"Looks like a brass button from a soldier's jacket, like the ones they wore during the Civil War." Now Stephen was sure they were on to something.

Cassie looked up at the sky again, "We'd better get back to Loft Mountain—it's starting to get dark. We can stop by the station and let the park rangers know what we found."

"I hate to admit it, but you're right. I wish we could keep this a secret until we can see what else is here, but it's better to let the rangers know. I'll take some close-up pictures of the canteen and the engraving on the butt of the rifle with my cell phone. I'm thinking it would be a good idea if we take the button with us to verify our story to the rangers."

Before heading back up to the trail, they covered the canteen and rifle with some branches. As Stephen and Cassie hiked back, they chatted about the artifacts they'd found. Did the rifle and canteen belong to an actual Civil War soldier? If so, what was he like? Was there a battle here? What was a soldier even doing in this part of Virginia?

Chapter Three

Stephen and Cassie soon arrived at the Loft Mountain clearing near the campground store, then walked up to the ranger station. As they entered the station, the ranger was bent over his desk, intent on reviewing his paperwork.

Stephen discreetly cleared his throat. The ranger looked up, seeming relieved to have some interruption from his work. He smiled, came out from behind his desk, and reached out his right hand toward them. "Hi! I'm Matt Shelbourne, park ranger on duty this summer at Loft Mountain. What can I do for you folks?"

Cassie filled him in on the details. "We were hiking down the Appalachian Trail toward Ivy Creek. Along the way, we took a 'detour' to the bottom of a hemlock hollow. We think we may have found some items belonging to a Civil War soldier."

Stephen took out his cell phone and showed Matt the photographs of the rifle and canteen. Matt's countenance became serious, his brows knitting together as he scrolled through the pictures on Stephen's cell phone.

"Interesting. The pictures are good of the rifle and canteen, but what makes you think these items belonged to a Civil War soldier?" asked Matt.

Stephen reached into his pocket, pulled out the gold-colored button Cassie found at the site, and handed it to the ranger. Matt looked it over silently. After a few moments, he raised his eyes and asked, "Could you locate the site again?"

Nodding his head, Stephen replied, "We should be able to find it without any problem."

Stephen showed Matt the approximate location on a park map. As they looked at the map, Cassie wondered, "Would it be possible to invite a friend of ours to look at the site, too? He's in anthropology and would be really interested. Also, he'd be helpful in doing a proper job of setting up the site as a potential anthropological dig, if it came to that."

Ranger Shelbourne replied, "I appreciate what you're saying, but if I know the Park Service, they'll want to make sure that if we're dealing with an historical site, the investigation is done properly. I'll call them right now."

He picked up the phone, dialed Park Service Headquarters, and informed them of the discovery, adding Cassie's proposal to have the site reviewed by their friend. He completed his conversation, then turned to face them. "Looks like you're in luck—Headquarters is OK with your friend coming. Contact him and see if he can be here first thing in the morning. Have him bring his resume and credentials and meet me here at the ranger station. It looks like Headquarters will be sending someone from Luray to meet with us."

"Why?" asked Cassie.

Matt explained, "It's just Park Service protocol. With all the downsizing they're doing and the backlog of work, they are contracting with universities and professionals familiar with doing this type of field work. I explained that your friend may be willing to serve as a contractor to oversee this work for us. Headquarters seems interested, but they want to make sure he has the credentials and background to oversee this project according to Park Service field research standards."

Stephen looked at Cassie. She squeezed his arm and nodded her head. Facing Matt, Stephen said, "Well, we'd like to continue working on this project, too. Is that OK?"

Matt outlined, "If your friend becomes the research contractor for this project, he can hire or allow access to whomever he pleases, as long as the work is done according to standard. I have to tell you both that the Park Service has strict guidelines. All items found at the site must be turned over to the Park Service. Any violation of this rule can cause your equipment and vehicle to be confiscated, and you could be subject to a large fine. While working as a contract employee, any original notes and photographs taken automatically becomes the property of the Park Service. Your friend will have to give me a report each evening summarizing all the activities surrounding the project. In turn, I have to forward it to Park Service Headquarters."

"Can we make copies of the notes and photographs?" Cassie asked.

"Yes, you can, but you cannot publish them in any form without first clearing it through the Park Service," said Matt.

"That seems a bit of an overkill." muttered Cassie.

Stephen assured her, "It makes sense, Cassie. We found the items on Park property. So, naturally, they're going to have their own rules for doing work on government land."

"I know you're right, but I don't have to like all the red tape" responded Cassie with her arms crossed.

Stephen retrieved his cell phone from Matt's desk, then called Daniel Gentry in Blacksburg, Virginia. Daniel had recently completed his graduate studies in anthropology in Florida, but was back in Virginia now. When Daniel heard about their discovery at Ivy Creek in the Shenandoah National Park, he excitedly agreed to come in the morning. Daniel said he'd also contact their son, JD, at Virginia Tech and see if he wanted to come along.

After ending the call, Stephen joined Cassie in completing

arrangements with Matt. After shaking hands with the ranger, they left the station.

Soon Stephen and Cassie were enjoying a late supper next to the campfire. While they cleaned up and put out the fire, they talking about the discovery and wondering what tomorrow would bring. Finally, the day's excitement took its toll, and they headed into their tent for the night.

Chapter Four

It was a short night, but Cassie and Stephen were up at dawn. They hastily dressed and ate a cold breakfast so they wouldn't need a fire. After a quick clean up of their camp site, they walked to the ranger's station. When they arrived, they were pleasantly surprised to see Daniel Gentry and their son, JD, already talking with Matt.

Matt motioned for Daniel to follow him inside the station, "I have some paperwork for you to fill out".

"What paperwork is he talking about?" JD asked Stephen.

"Basically, it's the contractual agreement between the Park Service and Daniel stating he is the one responsible for oversight on this project. He must ensure the work is professionally done according to best practices and that he and his staff will abide by Park rules and regulations with regard to doing the work on Federal property."

Cassie shook her head, "Still seems more complicated than it needs to be."

"It's necessary when dealing with the Federal government. They're responsible for preserving the integrity of the Park and its property," Stephen reminded her.

After about half an hour, Daniel came out of the station. "I brought my equipment and supplies in the back of my pickup, so we can properly set up and document the area. We'll gear up, then head down to Ivy Creek."

"Let's roll!" exclaimed JD.

At the pickup, each person got a backpack of equipment and supplies for the trek. Stephen led the small group down the Appalachian Trail toward Ivy Creek. Soon they were on the path where he'd slid down to the hollow below. Aware of Cassie's grinning, this time he carefully climbed down to the hollow's bottom. The others followed, then dropped their gear and supplies, listening as Daniel laid out how they would proceed.

Addressing Stephen, Daniel requested, "Show me where you found the rifle and the canteen." Stephen turned toward the creek and crossed to where they'd found the items. He removed the branches they'd left, motioning for Daniel to look. After a brief scan of the area, Daniel directed, "We need to set up the site for controlled digging. First, let's start putting up an 8 by 6-foot grid of twine on top of wooden stakes over the site where you originally found the items."

After starting Cassie and Stephen on setting up the grid, Daniel turned to JD and directed, "Use your Tablet to photograph the site and the items found in their original locations. Your Tablet takes really good, high-quality photographs, plus it will record accurate GPS data points for objects discovered on the site. At the end of each day, we'll download the photos and GPS data points into my laptop. I've got software that will generate an accurate site map documenting any pieces we find."

Nodding, JD picked up his Tablet and started photographing.

"Okay guys, " Daniel grinned as he addressed Cassie and Stephen, "Now comes the fun stuff. We each get a tiny masonry trowel and a 3-inch wide, soft-bristle paint brush to clear away the soil and debris in each grid section. If you find anything, stop what you are doing and call JD and me to come over to document the find."

Stephen marveled at how much technology had advanced since he was a student. Electronic tablets and laptops sure made the mapping and cataloging process a whole lot easier. He'd gone on one class dig in college just to see what it was like. They'd used brass transits and paper tablets -- with pencils!

After receiving instructions, the group worked their particular assignments with enthusiasm. The first discovery was made by Daniel while he was working the portion of the gridded area near the creek. He had brushed away debris to find the backside of a human skull. He stopped at once and called for everyone to come see what he'd found. They stared at the skull in silence, sobered by the fact that Daniel had found actual human remains. JD photographed the skull while Daniel tried to call Matt. "I just can't seem to get a signal down here in this hollow."

"I'll head up the trail until I can get a signal and give him a call," Stephen offered.

"Why do we have to call Matt?" Cassie asked, "Can't we just keep going since we're documenting what we find?"

Daniel explained, "Part of the contract I signed stipulates that if we find any remains that could be human, we are to notify Park Service immediately. It also stated that after notification, we can keep working until they provide instruction."

Stephen walked up the trail a few yards, but only got a weak signal on his cell phone. He shouted down to the group below, "I'm going to head further up the trail to try to get a signal. If worse comes to worse, I'll just walk up to the station and let Matt know what we found."

Cassie called back in response, "OK. Be careful!"

Stephen continued further up the trail in his quest for the elusive cell phone signal.

Soon the remaining group found several more bone fragments and artifacts. Each grid was meticulously sifted, brushed, and examined. JD recorded about three dozen bone fragments; some fabric remnants; buttons; a belt buckle; the rifle; the canteen; and a bugle-shaped, brass insignia. Daniel measured the site where the bone fragments were found and guessed that the person would have been about 5 and a half feet tall.

Stephen tried several more times to call Matt as he walked the trail toward the campground area. Finally, realizing he was less than half a mile away, he stopped trying to call and just headed for the ranger station. In a few minutes, he entered the station and found Matt drinking a cup of coffee while reading some sort of document. "Matt, we found something."

"What's up?" asked Matt.

"We found what we think is a human skull. Maybe it's a Civil War soldier." Stephen added.

"Or a victim of a recent homicide," Matt countered. "I'll call headquarters. I'm sure they'll want to know right away if there's any possibility this could be human remains."

Matt called Park Service headquarters. After a few minutes, he hung up the phone and looked at Stephen, "Two people from Park Police Headquarters are on their way here. We've been asked to wait for them and take them to the site. I'm guessing they'll be here in less than an hour."

"What do you want me to do?" asked Stephen.

"Just hang tight. I need you to lead us back down to where you guys are digging. In the meantime, I'll call Daniel and fill him in."

"Good luck in getting a signal down to them. I tried calling you several times while hiking from the hollow to the station, but there's just no cell phone reception down there."

Matt responded, "Let me try my phone. I have a different carrier out here." He tried calling Daniel on his cell, but could not get through to him. He then stepped outside the station and tried one more time, but still could not connect. Coming back inside, he admitted to Stephen, "I guess you're right. We'll just have to fill the group in when we get down there. We have a bit to wait; want a sandwich?"

"Yeah, that sounds fine."

Shortly, they heard the arrival of a vehicle. The door opened and two persons entered, explaining they were sent from Park Police. Matt filled them in, then asked Stephen to take them down to Ivy Creek. Matt stayed behind to man the ranger station.

The group in the hollow had been working since Stephen had left about two hours earlier. Cassie was getting worried since they hadn't heard from him during that time. Unspoken questions raced through her mind. "I wonder where he is? He's been gone for quite a while. What if something happened to him on the trail? I hope..."

Just then, she and the others heard voices coming from the trail, getting closer and closer. Eventually, she heard Stephen's voice, "Cassie! I'm coming!"

Stephen entered the hollow, leading a uniformed officer and a woman dressed in hiking clothes.

"I'm sorry it took so long, but I had to wait at the station until these folks from Park Headquarters came so I could lead them back here. This is Officer McDuffie from Park Police," he said pointing to the fortyish man in uniform. "And this is Joy Nighthawk from Park Headquarters," he added, introducing the younger, brown-haired woman.

The beautiful young woman smiled and started to say something, but was cut off when Officer McDuffie took charge, "All right now! Which of you is Daniel Gentry?"

Daniel stood up from where he was kneeling and firmly said, "I am."

"Good to meet you. It's obvious from the way the whole site

looks that you know how to set up a dig. Can you bring us up to date with what you've found so far?"

Daniel motioned for them to come closer toward the gridded area and confidently said, "Well, let's take a look at the site. It appears that the body was never buried, but was left to the mercy of the elements. Judging from the positioning of the skeletal remains, the body was face down on the ground originally. I don't think it just floated downstream during a storm, especially since we found a rifle and canteen right next to the remains."

He paused, "I think the person was shot and killed at this site. If he was a soldier, he must not have been involved in a major battle at the time of his death, or I would think they'd have recovered the body for burial. So whatever happened here, it probably occurred while he was apart from his company. I recommend that we dig deeper in the grid where we found the remains to see if we can find any more evidence. In my estimation, it looks like we still have more work to do to find any definitive answers."

Daniel continued, "Eventually, I would like to move the remains and artifacts we've found to a laboratory setting for further examination and analysis."

JD looked up at the reddish-purple sky. Turning toward the group he said, "It's getting dark. You'd best be heading back to the campground. Daniel and I are outfitted to camp here for the night. We plan to stay on site to make sure it's not disturbed."

Officer McDuffie looked at Daniel and said, "That will work. What you've done here so far looks good."

"Have you been keeping any notes or taken any photos?" asked Joy Nighthawk.

Daniel stiffly responded, "Of course. We've documented our work with notes and photos on JD's Tablet. When we're done with our work tonight, we will dock the Tablet to my laptop so I can run my mapping software for the site.

"Good. When you're done, can you make me a copy so I can download the information and photos to my computer?" Joy asked, pulling a flash drive from her backpack.

Daniel took the drive, but before he could respond, McDuffie called everyone together, "We'll be leaving now, but will be back first thing in the morning."

Everyone agreed it was time to call it a day. JD and Daniel began setting up their campsite while the others followed Stephen back toward the campground. As they hiked back, they agreed to meet early the following morning to return to the dig. Cassie also planned to take extra provisions for the duo camping in the hollow.

Chapter Five

Daylight was barely breaking when Stephen and Cassie filled two backpacks with water bottles, cooking utensils, and extra food. Shouldering their backpacks, they enjoyed the cool morning as they walked toward the ranger station to meet Matt, Officer McDuffie, and Joy Nighthawk.

Officer McDuffie greeted them with a change in plans. "I've got to return to Park Police Headquarters; however, Joy will stay here. I think you'll find her expertise in this type of work very beneficial." With that, he got in his vehicle and headed away from the ranger station.

Matt faced them, "Folks, I've got morning rounds of the campsites, so it looks like it's just you three going to Ivy Creek this morning." He saluted the trio, then turned toward the ranger station.

"Well... I'm ready, if you're ready!" said Joy with an infectious smile.

"Okay! Let's go!" agreed Stephen.

As the trio walked the trail toward the hollow, they saw several deer grazing quietly in open meadow areas. Their imaginations were stirred as they headed to the Ivy Creek area. What would they learn today?

As they approached the hollow, they saw JD and Daniel already busy at the gridded site. As the trio approached, JD greeted them, "Guess what, guys? We've already found a couple of bullets!"

"And take a look at this!" Daniel exclaimed. They went over to where he was sitting, examining now-exposed ribs and breast-bone. He showed them where a rib and the breastbone were notched and damaged.

"It looks like our soldier was shot at least twice. From the position of the notches on the bones, it's possible the bullets hit the bones as they passed through the body. Either shot wound could have been fatal."

"These aren't actually bullets," said Stephen, ever the Civil War buff. "They're called minié balls."

Daniel nodded, "OK - we'll be sure to document them correctly. At least, now we have evidence that this was the site where the soldier was shot and mortally wounded. I'm just wondering, is it possible to know more about what happened here?"

Ever the mother, Cassie asked Daniel and JD, "Have you guys had anything to eat this morning?"

JD grinned, "Yeah, we had a couple of granola bars and some water."

Cassie grimaced, "I figured as much." She ordered, "Stephen, would you please get a campfire going. I'm going to cook some real food for these guys!"

Smiling, Stephen got a fire going, knowing he'd have no peace until Cassie fed the young men. While she was getting a hearty breakfast ready, Daniel and JD showed Stephen and Joy where they'd found the minié balls. It wasn't long before the area smelled of coffee and fried potatoes with bacon and onions. The fragrant aroma of coffee and the sizzle of food cooking in an iron skillet soon drew everyone toward the fire. They pitched in to help Cassie in whatever way necessary so they could enjoy the mouth-watering food she was preparing. Soon they were settled around the fire with plates of heaping goodness. As they ate, they compared notes and thoughts about the discoveries.

"What will be your next step?" asked Joy.

Daniel responded, "With the distinct possibility that our soldier was shot here, it may prove fruitful to use the metal detector to scan beyond the gridded site for any other artifacts that may help us discover more about his story."

JD added, "Earlier this morning, we came up with several possibilities about what could have happened here. Judging from the placement of one of the minié balls we found, it's entirely possible that our soldier was shot from several yards above the hollow that direction." JD pointed to the top of the ridge across the creek from where they were sitting, adding "Maybe we can explore up there, too."

After finishing their breakfast and thanking the cook, the group was ready to tackle the day's work. Cassie volunteered to clean up while the rest worked on the project. Daniel assembled his metal detector and methodically walked the hollow bottom ground so that each square foot of ground was covered. Over the next few minutes, he found about a dozen minié balls, buried anywhere from a few inches to a foot into the ground. While Daniel was scanning the ground and making his discoveries, JD was shooting photos of the sites where the minié balls were found.

Stephen and Joy continued to excavate more in the grid. When she was done with clean-up, Cassie joined them. While brushing away loose soil, Cassie saw what seemed to be a flat piece of brass-colored metal. As she continued to brush away more soil, the object took the shape of a perfectly round disk. The disk had a concentric series of letters on the surface. She called to the group to come see what she'd found.

JD's face became animated when he saw the disk, "This looks like a device I've seen on some of the computer games I've played. It's some type of cipher." "What's a cipher?" asked Cassie.

Stephen shared his knowledge of Civil War history, "A cipher is a key used to code or decode a message. These types of devices were used during the Civil War on both sides. On the Union side, men entrusted with ciphers were working in concert with signal men on towers. A coded message would be sent via men using signal flags on top of the towers. The message would be written down and translated from code into military orders by the person trained to use the cipher. Our friend here was no ordinary soldier if he was carrying a cipher. More than likely, he was fairly well educated and very intelligent."

"Interesting, but what was he doing here?" asked Cassie.

"Well, we really don't know why he was here. Hopefully, as we continue our search, we will learn more about the soldier's story," replied Daniel.

Cassie responded, "Well then, I guess we'd better get back to work to see what else we can find out about him."

Finding the cipher spurred everyone on with renewed enthusiasm. Cassie, Joy, and Stephen continued to carefully excavate and brush away debris under the grid. JD documented the cipher find on his Tablet, and Daniel used his metal detector to finish scanning the site near the dried creek bed.

After Daniel had scanned the area thoroughly with no further finds, JD suggested, "Let's go to the top of the ridge where we think the shots may have been fired from to see if we can find anything up there."

Daniel looked toward the ridge and agreed, "Makes sense—we might find something useful up there."

Joy overheard their conversation, "I'm coming with you guys!"

They took their gear, crossed the dry creek bed, and proceeded to climb the ridge. Cassie and Stephen stayed at the bottom to work the grids. Cassie continued to work the section where she'd found the cipher. Even though Daniel had said it wasn't necessary to check the ground beyond the gridded site, Cassie had the nagging thought that she should go beyond the grid in that section. Stephen teased her about digging her way to China and affecting the surrounding ecosystem, but she just rolled her eyes at him and kept working. Stephen was pulled from his digging by Cassie's excited voice, "Stephen, look!"

Cassie was pointing at what looked like a dried up leather pouch. After Stephen used his cell phone to document the find, Cassie carefully picked up the pouch, "There's something small and hard inside, but I can't get it open."

She gave Stephen the pouch. He tried to open it, but time and the elements of nature had caused the pouch to shrivel and seal around the contents inside. He got the idea of wrapping the pouch in a wet cloth and warming it by the fire. He worked carefully so as not to damage the pouch or the contents inside.

After a few minutes of the spa treatment, the leather was still slightly stiff, but pliable enough to open. Carefully reaching inside the pouch, Stephen felt something hard and somewhat bumpy. After gingerly working the object out of the pouch, Stephen stared in amazement. Cassie had discovered a daguerreotype of a young woman! The Civil War Era photo was framed with pewter and appeared to be about two inches square. On the left side of the frame were two tiny metal hooks.

Cassie looked at the image of the young woman, and tears welled up in her eyes. Her voice trembled as she whispered, "I wonder if this was our soldier's wife or fiancée." His mind a million miles away, Stephen replied, "Could be... Could be."

On the other side of the creek, Daniel, Joy, and JD reached the point on the ridge where it would have been possible for someone to fire a rifle down at the soldier in the hollow. The top of the ridge was fairly level and heavily covered with trees and brush. They could see the remnant of a trail leading away from the ridge toward the main Appalachian Trail.

Daniel scanned the top of the ridge with his metal detector and found a couple of old metal bottle caps. Beyond that, they didn't find anything related to what had happened in the hollow below. Disappointed, they began to climb down the ridge. About half way down, JD saw a hole in the side of the ridge that he hadn't noticed on the way up.

"Daniel, do you have your flashlight? I want to take a look inside this hole."

Daniel grinned, as he handed the flashlight to JD. "You probably just found a hideout for skunks."

Grinning back, JD flicked on the flashlight and shined its beam into the hole. "It doesn't look like a skunk's den. It's much bigger than that. I can barely make out something inside— maybe some small barrels?"

He moved back and passed the flashlight to Daniel, "See what you think."

Daniel gazed inside, "I see what you're talking about over to the side of the cave, but can't make it out." He handed the flashlight to Joy and moved out of her way. She looked in the opening, "It does look like barrels, but I'm not totally sure either. The only way to know what's there is to go inside."

"Well, let's not worry about it right now," said JD. "so we get back down and let my folks know we didn't find anything along the top of the ridge."

They climbed the rest of the way down the ridge to where Cassie and Stephen were still looking at the daguerreotype.

JD quizzed, "What's that?"

Cassie declared, "We've found a pouch near the remains, and it contained this daguerreotype of a young woman."

She handed it to JD, who examined it carefully. With his

20-20 vision, he noticed a small notch at the corner of the frame. JD asked Stephen for his ever-present pocket knife, then used the small screwdriver to carefully pry in the notch. The back of the daguerreotype frame gave with a small pop and revealed the contents inside. "Would you look at this!" JD exclaimed.

Inside was a small lock of dark hair and a folded piece of paper. He gave the paper to Daniel who carefully unfolded it and read aloud the note that simply said, "LUNDY, with all my love. Mary."

Cassie sadly shook her head, "I bet she never knew what happened to him." Stephen slipped his arm around his wife's shoulders, hugging her close.

Changing mental gears, Cassie asked JD, "Did you guys find anything on top of the ridge?"

"No, we didn't find anything up top that would tie into our discoveries down here, but we did find something interesting coming back down the slope—a hole that seemed to lead to a large cave."

"Right, and we need to go back to that opening and look inside," Joy reminded him. "Remember what you said this morning about the trajectory of the minié balls? We have to think outside the box and consider the possibility that they could have come from the mouth of that cave." JD agreed, "You're right. Let's go take a look inside the cave."

"Hold on," said Cassie. "Lunch first. We'll have sandwiches and chips, then you three can go exploring," she smiled.

Everyone agreed, so Cassie got one of backpacks containing the extra food while the rest of the group got their drinks and chose seats on the ground. Daniel, JD, and Joy soon finished their sandwiches and prepared to return to the cave.

As the trio walked to the sloping ridge, Cassie turned to

Stephen and asked, "Do you remember when you used to be The Soldier Searcher?"

He nodded and smiled, guessing what she was about to ask him to do. Cassie continued, "Would you use your expertise in researching Civil War records to try to find out the identities of the soldier and the young woman in the daguerreotype?"

He put his arms around her and held her close. Looking into her eyes, he replied, "I'll do it, Cassie. It's the right thing to do."

She hugged him back, placing her head on his shoulder, "I just feel deep down that we need to do this. I can't explain it, but you understand, don't you?"

He quietly nodded his head.

She tilted her head to meet his eyes and whispered, "Thank you, Honey!"

Chapter Six

JD, Joy, and Daniel reached the hole in the side of the ridge. Joy stuck her head inside, her flashlight illuminating the open area beyond. "It looks like some sort of storage chamber. This could be something totally different than what we think it is -- maybe drug related. We won't know until we get these rocks out of the way and take a look inside."

Together, they wrestled the rocks and branches out of the way until the opening was large enough for them to enter the cave. Shining their flashlights around, they saw what originally had caught their attention—several small, wooden barrels about 2 feet tall. The seams of the barrels had been caulked with hemp rope, and the tops were made of wooden slats.

As JD and Joy held their lights above one of the barrels, Daniel began prying it open. His digging tool made the dry, wooden lid fairly easy to remove. Inside was some sort of black, powdery substance.

JD leaned over to smell the powder, "Smells slightly like sulfur."

Daniel wondered, "Maybe it's gunpowder. There's one way to find out."

With that, he took a portion of the powder and carried it out of the chamber into the open air. He placed the material on the ground, then stepped back a few feet. Taking out a match, he lit it, then tossed it onto the powder. Other than a brief fizzle, the material hardly burned at all.

Rejoining JD and Joy in the cave, Daniel noted, "Those are definitely gunpowder kegs, but the powder's gone bad. More than likely after years in this cave, it's become damp and useless."

As they continued examining the cave, JD found a small, round, cast iron pot. "That's odd. What would a crucible be doing here?" he puzzled.

"Whoever was here may have been melting down metal and pouring it into molds," replied Joy. Shining her light around the chamber again, she sighed, "The only problem with that theory is I don't see any metal in the cave."

JD took off his backpack, pulled out his Tablet, and began photographing the kegs and crucible inside the cave.

"All done. What now?" asked JD.

"Let's put the rocks and brush back over the opening and get back down to the dig site. If there's time, we can explore the cave more tomorrow," decided Daniel. "We need to regroup and decide what steps we need to take next."

Chapter Seven

With the group together again, Daniel said, "I think we've done all we can down here for the time being. Let's break camp and get everything we've found so far back to the ranger station.

JD and Daniel brought out the packing materials they had stored in one of the tents, while Joy told Stephen and Cassie about the items in the cave.

Daniel instructed everyone on how to pack the artifacts and skeletal remains. They knew it would probably take a couple of trips to get the camping gear and artifacts back to the Loft Mountain campground. Cassie, JD, and Joy each took a full load and began the hike back to Loft Mountain. Daniel and Stephen remained to take down the tents and break camp.

Back at the campground, Cassie decided to head to their campsite to prepare supper for all of them. Joy and JD took the artifacts to the ranger station, where Joy phoned in a report of the day's activities to Park Service Headquarters while JD filled Matt in on the day's activities. After completing her call, she and JD headed back down the Appalachian Trail.

When JD and Joy reached the hollow, they found everything packed and ready to go. Daniel said, "Looks like we can we can get the rest of this out in one trip." They each shouldered a backpack and hefted the remaining boxes, preparing to head back up the trail.

Stephen looked around at the hollow and pondered, "Finally, the soldier killed many, many years ago in this beautiful hollow is now able to leave it and head home, but where is home?"

"That's what we have to find out," replied Daniel.

Joy added, her voice indicating her conviction, "We owe it not only to the soldier, possibly left behind and forgotten by the army he served, but also to his family, who were unable to bring him home and probably never forgot him."

As they continued hiking toward Loft Mountain, Stephen pondered their finds and the possibilities. His reverie was broken by the sound of laughter at one of JD's witty tales. He smiled as he surveyed the young trio before him, glad they had come. He enjoyed learning from them—they had a lot to offer.

They arrived at the Loft Mountain ranger station and found Matt waiting for them. He showed them where they could secure all the artifacts and skeletal remains inside the building.

After thanking Matt, the tired and hungry group ambled over to the campsite where Cassie had prepared dinner. As they neared, their senses perked up from the sweet aroma rising out of the large cast iron pot resting on the fire.

Cassie asked Stephen to bring the pot to the table, then had everyone line up to serve themselves buffet-style. Needing little encouragement, Daniel led the way, filling his plate with luscious beef stew and biscuits. Cassie waited until the others had served themselves and were seated before she got her food and settled next to Stephen.

Before eating, Cassie and Stephen clasped hands as they'd done throughout their whole married life—no matter when or where. Stephen offered to the rest of the group, "You can join us in giving thanks for our food, if you'd like." Appreciatively, everyone bowed their heads. "Father, thank you for all the discoveries that have been made recently. Thank you for giving us our health, and thank you for this good meal we are about to share. Bless the hands that prepared it. Amen!"

During dinner, the discussion turned toward what to do next. So many discoveries had been made over the past two days, but many questions remained to be answered.

As they finished their dinner, Stephen asked Daniel, "What do we need to do so we can continue examining the artifacts and skeletal remains? Is there a plan of action that we need to follow?" Daniel nodded, "Yes, I figured we'd work on that next."

While JD helped Cassie get the dishes washed, Stephen helped Daniel and Joy put up their tents nearby. Afterward, the group gathered around the campfire, and Daniel opened the discussion on next steps the group should take.

JD stood up, went to his backpack, and pulled out his Tablet and keyboard. "Might as well document what we're going to do!" he said as he attached the Tablet to the keyboard on his knees. Over the next half hour, the group brainstormed about actions they should take to find answers to their many questions.

- Examine the skeletal remains and determine as much as possible about the soldier.

- Examine the artifacts found next to the remains; research Civil War records for matches.

- Explore deeper into the cave in the ridge. Determine if the cave has any ties with the soldier.

- Review historical documents/records to try to verify information about the soldier gleaned during the examinations/explorations.

- Document all information discovered.

- Provide report to Park Service Headquarters.

As JD read the list they had compiled, they determined what part of the project would suit each person based on particular interests and expertise. It soon became apparent that this was going to be a bigger job than their small group could handle.

"We're going to need more help if we're going to tackle this whole plan. Who else can we pull in to help us?" asked JD.

Nodding his head, Daniel impishly grinned and leaned toward Cassie and Stephen, "Think it's time for a pinochle game?"

They laughed. Cassie and Stephen knew exactly what he meant. Cassie got out her cell phone and tapped in a number. A voice answered at the other end, "Hello, this is Lisa." Cassie smiled, "Hey, pinochle partner! Would you and Tim be willing to come to Loft Mountain tomorrow? We could use your help on an unusual project."

Lisa asked, "What kind of unusual project?"

Cassie took several minutes to explain to Lisa about their find near Ivy Creek, sweetening the pot with the fact that Daniel, Lisa and Tim's son, was already here. Lisa's excitement grew. "Tim and I will definitely meet you at Loft Mountain tomorrow morning!"

"Great! We'll meet you at the front entrance near the ranger station! Don't forget the pinochle cards!" chuckled Cassie.

Chapter Eight

As morning broke the following day, the blue mist covered the tents and grass with a light dew. A damp coolness pervaded the air as Stephen woke up inside the tent. He gently shook Cassie's arm and said, "I'm getting dressed, and then I'll walk down to the campground entrance to wait for Tim and Lisa."

"Ok, I'm getting up, Honey," Cassie mumbled, then promptly fell right back to sleep. Stephen grinned as he put on his boots, figuring he'd wake her up when he got back. He knew she wasn't a morning person, despite the excitement of the previous few days.

He exited the tent, making sure to zip down the flaps to keep out small critters and insects. Glancing at JD's campsite and seeing no campfire or activity, he assumed the trio had already gone up to the ranger station to meet with Matt.

As he ambled down the winding road to the main entrance, Stephen was struck by the serenity and beauty before him. The deer browsing in open fields throughout the campground completed the picture-perfect morning. At one point, he enjoyed a comical scene as two squirrels climbed inside a trash can, then popped back up with apple cores to munch while perched on the wooden rim of the trash container. They definitely had been imprinted by human presence, he mused.

Almost to the main entrance, Stephen realized that Tim and Lisa Gentry were already there, waiting for him. After a warm welcome, Lisa asked, "Where's Cassie?"

Stephen chuckled, "Still sound asleep. I'll get her up when we get back to our campsite. We made arrangements for y'all to have the campsite next to us. If I can ride with you, I'll show you which site it is."

"Sounds good!" Tim agreed.

After a short drive down the narrow road, Tim parked in the site next to Stephen and Cassie. Lisa was the first one out of the car with "I'm going to check on Cassie," leaving Tim and Stephen to unpack the car and set up the campsite.

Lisa unzipped Cassie's tent flap and bent down to reach inside. She gently shook Cassie's leg, "Cassie! We're here!"

Cassie awoke with a start, then sat up and smiled as she reached out to hug Lisa. She apologized for not meeting them at the entrance, but Lisa laughingly reassured her it was all right. Cassie asked Lisa if she wanted to go with her to the women's bathhouse to freshen up a bit after their trip.

Tim and Stephen chuckled as they watched Lisa and Cassie head toward the bathhouse, clearly enjoying each other's company. Looking around the campsite, Stephen said to Tim, "Before you set up your tent, let's find some wood so we can get a fire going."

Tim agreed, and they scavenged the area for dry branches and small sticks. They soon had enough material to start a decent fire.

As they watched the flames catch hold and grow, Stephen asked, "Have y'all had any breakfast yet, Tim?"

"We had some cereal and juice before we left the house," he replied.

"How about you and I get some pancakes going and have them ready when Cassie and Lisa get back?" grinned Stephen. Tim smiled back in agreement. While Stephen went to get the food from his campsite, Tim set out the griddle and cooking utensils.

With everything now at hand, Tim mixed up the batter, and Stephen got the griddle heated and ready for pancakes. Stephen manned the griddle, so Tim set the picnic table with paper plates, forks, and drinks. Cassie and Lisa came back just as Tim placed the steaming platter of pancakes on the table.

The four close friends sat down to a wonderful breakfast reunion, catching up on current events within their families. They'd known each other for so long, over 20 years now, that they were more like family than friends.

Stephen thought back—they'd first met Tim and Lisa when all their kids were in grade school, except Daniel, who was still a toddler. Since the oldest child from each family was in the same grade at school, they soon found themselves together at many functions.

When Tim and Lisa bought a house down the street from Stephen and Cassie, their friendship was cemented. While the kids played together outside, the adults played inside—pinochle, of course.

As they were finishing up, Tim asked, "Where do we need to go after breakfast?"

Stephen replied, "Once we get the dishes cleaned up and the food put away, we'll walk up the hill toward the ranger station."

Stephen could tell both Tim and Lisa were really excited and could hardly wait a moment more, but it didn't take long to clean up and put out the fire. Soon the four friends were walking toward the ranger station, enjoying the sun's warm, yellow rays stretching through the canopy of trees.

At the station, JD, Daniel, and Joy were already inside talking with Matt. Matt welcomed Tim and Lisa and spent a few minutes getting acquainted. Daniel soon took charge, "Everyone, please take a seat, and we'll get started."

Lisa was startled by Daniel's authoritative tone, but Tim quietly assured her, "Lisa, we have to remember that Daniel's in charge of this project and we're here to help. With his background, he definitely knows more than we do about this type of work."

Everyone positioned themselves so they could hear what Daniel had to say. He started by presenting a hypothesis, "It is entirely possible that we have found the remains of a Civil War soldier. Based on that premise, each person around the table will be fulfilling an essential role in the research to find the identity of the soldier and why he was at Ivy Creek. Yesterday, JD took some notes while we were developing an action plan. Would you mind sharing those, JD?"

JD found the file on his Tablet, then read the notes from the day before. When JD was done, Daniel posed two questions to the group: "What can we learn from the skeletal remains? And what can we learn from examining the artifacts found near the remains?"

The two questions seemed very simple - or so they thought. But how were they going to find the answers? After much discussion, they formed objectives and decided to break up into two groups. The first objective of learning as much as possible from the skeletal remains would be handled by Daniel, JD, Matt, and Joy. The second objective of researching the artifacts would be tackled by Cassie, Lisa, Tim, and Stephen.

Chapter Nine

Daniel, JD, Matt, and Joy separated their objective into two segments: 1) what the skeleton could tell them about the height and build of the man, and 2) the possibility of using computer modeling to simulate how the man would have looked when alive.

Daniel asked Matt, "Where can we lay out the skeleton exactly as we found it in the field?"

Matt offered, "There's a large table in the back storage room. Do you think that would that do it?"

"Let's try it and see," replied Daniel.

Using the photographs taken by JD, the four carefully laid out the bones as they had been found in the field -- face down. They stood back and looked at the skeleton on the table, then decided to lay out the skeleton as if the person were sleeping on his back to make measuring easier. The rearranging completed, Daniel and Joy took several dozen measurements of the skeleton, with JD recording them on his Tablet. Daniel reviewed the data and stated, "These measurements confirm what we thought in the field. It looks like he stood around 5 feet, 6 inches tall, which was actually average for a soldier in that time period. His chest would have been about a size 38, and he had relatively narrow shoulders. Judging from the amount of wear on the leg joints, it appears that he was average in weight—say 135 pounds."

"Leg joints?" asked Matt.

Daniel explained, "If there was a lot of grinding on the

bone at the joints, more than likely the man would have been heavy-set in life, but we don't see that here. The wear on these joints indicate that he was physically in good shape."

After examining the condition of the skull and the wear on the teeth, Daniel concluded, "I would say this man was somewhere between 22 to 26 years old when he was killed."

"Daniel, show Matt how you think our buddy may have been killed," said JD.

Nodding agreeably, Daniel began, "I would say he died from several bullet wounds to both his front and back."

"How can you tell that?" asked Matt.

Daniel continued, "Look at this rib. See the nick? Some object or projectile caused impact damage predominantly on the front of the rib and very little on the back of it."

"That makes sense, but how can you tell he was also shot in the back?" asked Matt.

Daniel turned over the rib cage and pointed to where another rib had been shattered. He gave Matt a magnifying glass and instructed him to look closely at the shatter point on the rib.

Daniel explained, "You can see there is significant damage to this rib near where it attached to his spine. This is typical damage to the bone when a person is shot in the back."

"So our soldier friend was probably shot both in the front and in the back. Either wound would have been fatal. Based on the location of the two damaged ribs, the heart and lungs would have been compromised."

Matt responded, "Whew! That's amazing!"

Daniel continued, "Take a look at the tarsal bones in the hand—you can see where several bones were shattered. The soldier was probably wounded in the hand as well."

"From what you're saying, it sounds like our friend here may have been surrounded when he was shot," Matt said thoughtfully.

JD added, "I can't imagine how he fought back if he was outnumbered."

"Well, right now, we can only speculate as to what actually happened to him at Ivy Creek. We need more facts," said Daniel.

"Okay, now that we have a good idea of what killed the soldier, what's the next step?" asked Matt.

JD eagerly replied, "Seem like this would be a good time to try facial reconstruction using computer technology."

Daniel grinned, "I'm very familiar with the process, but we'll have to find a place with the computers and programs to do that type of work."

Joy had been quiet up to this point, but now shared, "I know a place—my lab at the university."

Daniel and JD looked at her in surprise. Daniel spoke first, "What? Why didn't you say something before? We thought you were law enforcement with the Park Service!"

"No, I am a contractor just like you are, Daniel. Actually, I'm a forensic specialist. I, too, am quite familiar with that process," she said grinning. "In my lab, I use laser-based scanning equipment and specialized programs to develop computer images and make 3-D models using plasticine materials. Park Service has hired me several times over the past few years to help solve mysteries like this one," she added.

"Wow! I had no clue that you possessed this type of background," replied Daniel.

Joy smiled and responded, "You never asked; you just assumed."

"You're right, Joy. My apologies—I should have asked about your background and expertise," responded Daniel sheepishly. He caught JD's eye—they were thinking the same thing. They had definitely underestimated the beautiful young woman standing before them.

JD quickly jumped in, "Joy, would you be willing to use your skills to help us?"

Joy confidently agreed, "That shouldn't be a problem. In fact, I did a job similar to this very recently. A neurosurgeon contacted me to see if I could develop a plasticine model of a brain. He wanted to study a life-like replica prior to operating on one of his patients. I guided him through the process of scanning his patient's brain. He then sent me the information electronically so I could make the model."

JD looked at Joy and asked, "Cool! We don't need a plasticine model of the skull, just the computer rendition. Say, is it possible to do a computer-generated reconstruction of an entire body? Like a way to 'humanize' the entire skeleton?"

Joy replied, "Yes, it's possible."

Daniel spoke up, "We would definitely like to use your lab. I'll cover any costs under my contract with the Park Service." JD and Matt nodded their heads in agreement.

After carefully packing the skeleton, they loaded them boxes into Daniel's pickup truck. Matt told the trio, "As park ranger for Loft Mountain, I'll have to stay at my post. Here are my cell phone number and e-mail address. Please keep me informed. Meanwhile, I'll let the rest of the group know where you're headed and see if I can do anything to help them with the other artifacts here."

JD, Joy, and Daniel got into the pickup truck and started down the highway for Blacksburg, Virginia—home of Virginia Tech University.

By late afternoon, they had arrived at Daniel's apartment on the outskirts of Blacksburg. As a precaution, they secured all the boxes inside his apartment before going to a nearby restaurant for dinner. After an enjoyable meal, Daniel drove JD and Joy to their apartments, having made arrangements to pick them up the following morning. Tomorrow, they would go to Joy's lab.

Shortly after sunrise, Daniel loaded the boxes into his pickup truck, securing them under a tarp, then drove to pick up the others.

When the three were together again, Daniel asked, "Have you all had anything to eat this morning?"

JD replied, "I had a granola bar. Does that count?"

"Figures," grinned Daniel. "I haven't eaten yet. Would you like to get something to eat on campus?"

"Sounds good to me. Squires should be open this time of morning," said Joy.

With everyone in agreement, Daniel turned off Prices Fork Road, onto West Campus Drive, and headed for the Drill Field. He knew that he could find parking near Squires since it was summer and the majority of the students were gone.

All three were quite familiar with the campus, making conversation easy during their drive. They passed many familiar buildings constructed of the signature black, gray, and white limestone blocks with hand-chiseled facades. Daniel continued to drive to the Drill Field where he knew there would plenty of parking spaces this early in the day.

After parking, they walked toward the library plaza. Squires was on the left just beyond the library. They went inside heading for the only place open for breakfast.

"You know," JD quipped, "this is a lot better than the granola bar I had this morning." Daniel and Joy laughed, knowing that it wouldn't be long before JD would be thinking about lunch. The trio chatted easily as they finished their meal.

Finally, Daniel said, "Well, I guess we should be going— we've got a job to do. Joy, where's your lab?"

"It's out in Research Park off Tech Center Drive. I'll have to show you which building when we get there," said Joy.

They left Squires and walked back to Daniel's truck. Soon they were on their way to the other side of the campus, not too far from the airport. As they turned off Tech Center Drive into the Research Park, Joy pointed out the building where her lab was located.

After parking the truck, they unloaded the boxes.

Joy used her pass key to enter the building, then led the way to the lab where she did her work. Again using her pass key, Joy entered the lab and held the door for Daniel and JD, then showed them where to place their boxes.

Daniel opened the box he had been carrying, and Joy gingerly lifted out the skull. After thoroughly examining it, she nodded, "It shouldn't be a problem to scan the skull and do the computerized reconstruction process, but it will take a few hours to complete. Fortunately, we got the lab at a time when there aren't too many projects going on."

She added, "The first thing I need to do is scan in the skull." She positioned the skull on a rotating pedestal, then meticulously set up the optical laser scanning equipment. Once the setup was complete, she began scanning the skull and downloading the measurements into her computer.

After completing the scan, Joy looked over to Daniel and JD, "With the information we just gathered, it should be easy to interface with the department's new facial typology computer program."

Joy led them to another work station, and Daniel came around the desk. After looking at the large screen, he told Joy, "I'm very familiar with this program. I used it when I was in grad school down in Florida."

Joy looked up at Daniel and grinned, "Since you're that familiar with the program, you can run it, if you'd like."

She got up and motioned for Daniel to sit down. Joy and

JD watched over Daniel's shoulder as he began to deftly use the keyboard and program to rotate the skull on the screen and add facial features to it. Soon the trio was viewing the face of a bald Caucasian male.

At that point, Daniel stated, "He needs some hair. What color do you think?"

"We know he was a young man, and the odds are good that he probably had medium to dark-brown hair," offered JD. "More than likely, the hair would be trimmed around the ears and above the eyebrows. The eyebrows would be dark, but not too bushy."

Daniel imported dark brown hair onto the scalp and added eyebrows that would typically be found on a young man.

When the discussion turned to mustaches and beards, they decided to have three different images—one with no facial hair, one with a trimmed mustache, and one with a trimmed beard.

When all three images were complete, they decided to add the body dimensions to the head to show a full body. With masterful strokes on the keyboard, Daniel was able to create a computerized image of what the entire man may have looked like in real life. Now, it was up to the other team members to determine the identity of the man and what he did during the Civil War.

With a great deal of satisfaction, Daniel looked at Joy and JD, "Let's download everything and get something to eat before we head back to Loft Mountain."

They thanked Joy for her help, then Daniel asked, "How much do we owe you for the use of your lab?"

"It will cost you exactly one lunch," laughed Joy.

"Sounds good to me," JD said enthusiastically. "Let's eat! This time, we'll go to one of my favorite off-campus spots!"

Chapter Ten

Matt walked inside the station to where Stephen, Tim, Cassie, and Lisa were already itemizing what had been found at the site. The list included:

- the rifle;

- several brass buttons with a torch centered between two crossed flags;

- a daguerreotype of a young woman found inside a leather pouch (The daguerreotype had shielded a note declaring, "To LUNDY, with all my love. Mary".);

- a canteen;

- a brass cipher;

- a belt buckle with the raised letters "US" in the center;

- fragments of dark-blue cloth; and

- several minié balls, including those that may have killed the young man.

Tim lifted the rifle to examine the wooden stock, while Stephen pointed out the hand-carved Masonic symbol and initials, E.L.D., on the rifle butt.

Tim acknowledged, "With these clues, we can surmise that our friend, E.L.D., was a Mason, but will that be enough information to help us determine his full identity?"

"I wonder if identifying the make and model of the rifle would be helpful?" queried Stephen. I'm sure There are several on-line sites that deal with Civil War rifles."

Tim and Stephen began searching the internet for rifles used during the Civil War. After perusing several different sites, they found a web page filled with color photographs of rifles, including an 1859 model Sharps breech loading rifle.

Tim nodded his head, "I think we've found it. From what I am reading here, it was the chosen rifle used predominantly by the 1st and 2nd U.S. Sharpshooters of the Union Army—also known as Berdan's Sharpshooters."

Stephen responded, "I remember reading about them a few years ago. Each member of this elite group had to demonstrate excellent marksmanship before he could be called a sharpshooter. Could it be that our soldier was a member of Berdan's Sharpshooters?"

Tim picked up the rifle again. As he flipped over the rifle butt, he noticed a small metal compartment with a lid inset into the wood. He tried to pry the lid open, but it didn't budge; obviously, the hinge was badly corroded. Tim looked up and asked Matt, "Got any spray lubricant?"

Matt replied, "Sure! I've got a can out in my truck tool box. Be right back."

Matt returned quickly with the lubricant. Tim sprayed it on the hinge and allowed it to soak. After a few moments had passed, Tim carefully worked the lid up and down several times until the lid could be opened completely. Inside, he discovered a small compartment containing a folded piece of yellowed paper. Tim gingerly unfolded it and silently read what was written on the paper. Puzzled, Tim looked up and passed it to Stephen, "What do you make of this?"

After a few minutes of trying to decipher the message, Stephen passed it to Matt, stating, "Wow! The way the message reads now, it just doesn't make any sense. I wonder if it could be some sort of a code."

Matt looked at the message and just shook his head, handing it back to Tim.

While the men were examining the rifle, Cassie and Lisa were doing their own research on the buttons and daguerreotype. Using Cassie's laptop, they searched for websites dealing with Civil War buttons. Lisa sat beside Cassie hoping that an extra set of eyes would help with the search.

After several minutes of viewing web pages with photographs of Civil War buttons, Cassie and Lisa excitedly leaned toward the screen. They had spotted a photograph of the same button found in the hollow. The button was worn on the service jacket of men belonging to the U.S. Signal Corps.

With that information, they started searching for information on the U.S. Signal Corps during the Civil War. They were amazed to discover that the men in the Signal Corps had come from all parts of the country. They were intelligent men with experience in telegraphy, communications, and cryptography or cryptology.

Lisa looked over to the table where the cipher was located and said, "This is starting to make sense now! It's very possible that we have a man who was a member of the U.S. Signal Corps during the Civil War. Is it possible to find a roster of some sort on the Web so we can check to see if someone is listed with the initials E.L.D.?"

Agreeing, Cassie began to search for a roster of the U.S. Signal Corps during the Civil War. After searching for several minutes, she came across a website that listed all of the officers and enlisted men who had served in the U.S. Signal Corps during the Civil War and where they had enlisted. As they scanned the list, they came across two names that matched the initials E.L.D. found on the rifle butt—Elias L. Dixon and Edward L. Doherty.

Elias had enlisted in the military in 1862 from Pennsylvania, and Edward had enlisted in 1862 from Michigan. Cassie looked up at Lisa and said, "It's going to take more digging to determine which of the two men it could be."

Lisa replied, "Stephen used to have a business tracking down Civil War ancestors, right? Maybe he could tell us how to proceed with this type of research."

They got up from their chairs and went to where the guys were examining the folded document found inside the rifle's small compartment. Lisa spoke up, "Cassie and I think we may have found two possible identities for the soldier."

Cassie shared, "We compared the brass buttons with photos on the Web and discovered they were U.S. Signal Corps buttons. Our soldier was probably a member of the U.S. Signal Corps during the war."

Matt spoke up, "Well, we thought the soldier was actually part of Berdan's Sharpshooters. Now it appears there were two possible units that could claim this soldier as a member."

"Hold on, Matt," Tim interjected, "According to what we found inside the rifle's compartment, I am inclined to agree with Lisa and Cassie."

Matt responded, "Are you sure?"

Tim stated, "It makes sense, if you think about it. What Cassie and Lisa found on the internet strengthens the argument that the document we found inside the rifle compartment is written in some sort of code. We'll just have to figure out is what type of code system the soldier was using when he wrote this message."

"What message?" asked Cassie.

Stephen showed Cassie and Lisa the note they had found. "Tim found this message inside a compartment in the rifle butt."

After trying to read the message for a few minutes, Cassie shook her head, "It doesn't make any sense!"

Lisa looked at Tim and asked, "Do you know how to go about deciphering the message?"

He cocked his head to the side and looked thoughtfully into the air for a few moments. Shaking his head, he looked at the group, "If this was one of those puzzles you find in a newspaper, I could probably figure it out. This one has me stumped."

Lisa asked, "Do you think this brass thing that JD called a brass cipher could be used to decipher the message?"

Tim's face lit up as he replied, "It's a distinct possibility!"

"But how do we use it?"

Tim responded, "Good question. Guess we better do some research on ciphers and decoding messages during the Civil War."

Matt offered, "I can call the Park Service library in Front Royal to see if they have any information about Civil War codes."

Stephen raised his hand, "Decoding the message is important, but right now I think we should focus on learning more about the two men Cassie and Lisa found on the Signal corps roster. It's highly likely that their service and pension records could provide clues to identify our soldier."

Looking to Cassie, he asked, "What are the names of the two men you and Lisa found?"

Cassie answered, "Elias L. Dixon from Pennsylvania, and Edward L. Doherty from Michigan."

Stephen responded, "With names and states of residence, it should be relatively easy to find the records of these two men at the National Archives in Washington, DC."

Cassie looked at him and asked, "Would you mind going to DC to search for their records?"

Stephen replied, "No, I don't mind going. It's been a few years since I did this type of work. Hopefully, it shouldn't be any problem finding their records. I'll head out early tomorrow morning. In the meantime, let's see if we can find any information on Civil War codes."

For the rest of the afternoon, Matt made his rounds of the campground, while Stephen went to the Park Service library to do research. Tim, Lisa, and Cassie stayed at the ranger station using their laptops to peruse sites on Civil War codes.

After several hours of research, they reunited for supper at Stephen and Cassie's campsite. The guys got a fire started, while Lisa set the picnic table, and Cassie quickly made drop biscuits to go with the canned chili she'd brought.

When everyone was seated, Stephen asked Tim, "Would you mind giving thanks for our meal tonight?"

They joined hands and bowed their heads. Tim prayed, "Father, we thank You for what we have discovered so far today. We feel a sense of inadequacy as we try to decipher the message found inside the rifle compartment. We need Your help in figuring out what to do. Please be with Stephen tomorrow as he travels to D.C. and with Daniel, JD, and Joy down in Blacksburg. We ask for Your continued blessing and guidance as we proceed with our work. We ask this in Christ's name. Amen!"

The group felt a sense of quiet assurance and renewal. That good feeling was strongly reinforced with plenty of warm food and pleasant company.

Chapter Eleven

Stephen woke before dawn the following morning and tried not to disturb Cassie while she slept. However, with limited space to dress inside the tent and him rustling around, she woke up and sleepily asked, "Do you want me to get up and fix some breakfast for the both of us?"

He gave her a kiss and whispered, "That would be nice! I'll get the fire going."

While she was getting up, Stephen went outside to start a campfire. Within a few minutes, the flames died down to red-hot embers, making it ideal to brew a pot of coffee. If there was one thing he always enjoyed, it was the aroma of fresh hot coffee on a cool morning.

Before long, Cassie came out of the tent, and they sat down near the campfire to savor hot coffee and pastry. After finishing their breakfast, Cassie assured Stephen she'd be fine while he was gone to D.C. Tim and Lisa were right here if she needed anything. Stephen gave Cassie a warm parting kiss before he got into their car. He waved out the window and started driving down the mountain toward Vienna so he could catch the Metro Rail to the National Archives.

Within a few hours, he pulled into the Vienna Metro Rail station and parked the car. After purchasing his pass at the kiosk, Stephen stood on the platform anxiously awaiting the train. It wasn't long before the round lights in the platform began blinking methodically to let him know a train was coming. The train rumbled into the station and screeched to a stop. The doors opened, and he boarded along with dozens of other commuters. Stephen began to relax as he sat down in a seat next to a window.

After several above-ground stops, the train started to dive underground into a tunnel. Eventually the train went underneath the Potomac River. It wasn't long before Stephen reached a transfer station. He got off the train and walked to another platform to catch the Red Line train. Within a few minutes, he was at the Metro station for the National Archives. Stephen exited the Metro station and walked the short distance to the impressive building.

It had been a few years since he'd done genealogical research at the Archives. Stephen signed in at the security podium where they inspected his backpack. Then he went to the front desk and filled out the necessary form to apply for a genealogical researcher's card. After receiving his card, he went to the fourth floor where the United States census records and military records were available on microfilm and microfiche for researchers. Many of the research stations were already taken; but, after looking around the facility, Stephen found a microfilm reading machine in an isolated corner that he could use. He opened his backpack and pulled out a notebook and pen. Then he started searching several rows of microfilm cabinets for the pension files and service records of Elias L. Dixon and Edward L. Doherty.

After finding two possible microfilm reels, Stephen went back to his microfilm reading machine and placed the reel with the searchable index for Union service records on the spindle and slid the microfilm between the lenses. After turning on the machine light to see, he cranked the microfilm reel to where he found both Elias and Edward. Stephen wrote down the index information found for both men.

- Private Elias L. Dixon, Co. B, 141 Pennsylvania Infantry and U.S. Signal Corps

- Private Edward L. Doherty, Co. E, 20 Michigan Infantry and U.S. Signal Corps

After rewinding the reel, he inserted the next microfilm reel that contained Union pension record indexes. Stephen scrolled for a few minutes before finding the pension application information for both men. He was surprised by what was written on the index for Private Edward L. Doherty. It looked like Private Doherty was killed in 1864 and his wife, Mary Doherty, had applied for a widow's pension. Maybe this was their soldier since the note in the daguerreotype they'd found had been signed by a Mary. However, the index had something Stephen had not seen before. Her application for a widow's pension had been rejected. Intriguing!

Knowing there was more information to be had, Stephen wanted to view the actual documents contained in the service and pension application records for both soldiers. Going back to the service desk, he filled out four request forms to view the two sets of service records and the two sets of pension records for Privates Dixon and Doherty. He handed the requests to the librarian who let him know that it would be about an hour before the files would be available and to pick them up at the circulation desk on the second floor.

Stephen went down to the second floor. While waiting, he browsed some of the military volumes housed there. After the hour was up, he went to the circulation desk to pick up four large, brown envelopes. Choosing a table in front of a photocopier, he sat down to view the original documents concerning both men. Stephen picked up the service record for Private Dixon and read through his file. It seemed fairly standard. He had enlisted in 1862 and was mustered into service at Harrisburg, Pennsylvania. Near the end of 1862, he had volunteered to serve as a telegrapher for the U.S. Signal Corps in Washington, D.C. He served primarily in the D.C. area for the duration of the war. The only battle action he had seen was in 1864 when Lt. General Jubal Early and his army attacked the Union troops at Monocacy, Maryland.

Based on archive protocols, Stephen knew he needed to process each envelope separately so records did not get filed out of order or placed in the wrong envelope, so he turned to the machine behind him to make copies of Private Dixon's service records, Stephen carefully placed the original records back into their envelope, then opened another large envelope containing Dixon's pension records.

Stephen was always amazed when he looked at the pension records for Union soldiers. He never knew what he'd find as reasons for obtaining a federal pension. In Private Dixon's case, he'd requested a pension because he had recurring headaches after a fellow soldier had accidently clubbed him on the head with his rifle during marching drill exercises in 1862. As a result of that injury, Dixon was granted a pension of $10 a month.

As Stephen continued reading more about Private Dixon, it dawned on him that the remains of the soldier they'd found in Shenandoah National Park could not have been Private Dixon!

Based on Private Dixon's pension records, he had survived the war and returned to his farm outside of Harrisburg, Pennsylvania, where he died in 1899. So the remains they'd found couldn't have been Dixon. Stephen photocopied some of the documents in the pension file and returned Private Dixon's service and pension records to the circulation desk.

Stephen opened the service record of Private Edward L. Doherty, Co. E, 20 Michigan Infantry, hoping it contained the proof he needed. Doherty had enlisted in August 1862 in Jackson, Michigan. Shortly after his enlistment, Doherty demonstrated extraordinary skill in marksmanship and was encouraged to try out for Berdan's Sharpshooters. In October, he was accepted as a sharpshooter and was placed in Berdan's 1st U.S. Sharpshooters. He participated in several minor skirmishes and his sharpshooting skills earned him a commendation for rendering a battery of cannons ineffective during the Gettysburg Campaign.

After Gettysburg, Doherty volunteered to serve in the U.S. Signal Corps. He was recognized by his superiors as a master telegrapher—so good, in fact, that they trained him to be a cryptographer. The more Stephen read about Private Doherty, the more he felt that Doherty was the man whose remains they'd found in the hemlock hollow near Ivy Creek.

As Stephen continued to read through the service records, he found several documents containing details about Doherty deserting to the enemy and providing them with military information deleterious to the Union Army.

There was an account written in 1864 by a Lieutenant Purdy, stating that Private Doherty was a traitor to the Union and that he had been tracked down in the Shenandoah Valley by Purdy and his men. Doherty was surrounded and ordered to surrender, but refused, so he was fired upon and killed by Purdy. Stephen whispered, "Wow! What did I just find here?! I expected him to have been killed in battle, not by fellow Union soldiers! What happened?"

Stephen photocopied the entire service record of Private Doherty. After putting the original documents back into the large, brown envelope, he proceeded to open the envelope containing Doherty's pension files. Stephen took his time, reading each page thoroughly.

The fifth page was a fragile family document showing the date and place of the marriage of Edward L. (for Lundawick) and Mary Doherty. Immediately Stephen though about the names of Lundy and Mary on the back of the daguerreotype Cassie had found in the hollow. Could it be that Lundy was a nickname for Lundawick?

As Stephen perused the entire set of historical documents, he came across two applications for a Federal pension by the widow, Mary Doherty. She applied for a widow's pension in 1864 and again in 1866, but was denied because of the three eyewitness testimonies of Lieutenant Lucius Purdy, Sergeant Benjamin Carmichael, and Corporal Amos Devereaux, stating that Private Doherty was a traitor who had provided information to the enemy. Incredible!

Initially, it appeared that Private Edward L. Doherty was quite a soldier -- a highly regarded sharpshooter and cryptographer -- and now because of these damning testimonies, his widow was denied any type of pension support by the U.S. Government. Which version was true -- honorable soldier or traitor?

Stephen photocopied the entire pension file, returned the originals to their envelope, and placed the photocopies into his backpack. He had hoped to find an interesting story of a typical Civil War soldier, but instead he'd uncovered a mystery that opened many more questions.

Stephen returned Doherty's service and pension records to the circulation desk. He looked at his watch and was surprised to see it was already mid-afternoon. His pace quickened as he secured his notes and photocopies inside his backpack.

Instead of taking the slow elevator, Stephen walked down the steps to the first floor and exited the Archives. He walked to the subway entrance and took the escalator down to the subway train platform where he purchased his fare card from the machine. His hope was to beat most of the rush hour crowd boarding the Metro Rail.

Within a few moments, he saw the flashing platform lights and heard the familiar rumble of the subway train. As it screeched to a stop, the doors opened, and Stephen boarded and sat down next to a window. He breathed a sigh of relief that the train was not crowded. His stomach reminded his that he'd missed lunch. Checking his backpack, he found a granola bar left from the last time he'd hiked. Smiling contentedly, Stephen settled back to enjoy the ride and his snack.

The train stopped several times along the way, but within thirty minutes, he'd arrived at the Vienna station. Stephen wanted to get on the road before rush hour traffic got too heavy, so he quickly got in his car and exited the parking lot.

Heading back to Loft Mountain, he pondered what would make a fine, upstanding soldier turn traitor. The evidence he'd found at the Archives seemed to reinforce this harsh judgment call. After driving about an hour, a different thought popped into Stephen's mind–is it possible that Doherty wasn't really a traitor? If not, what happened that caused those three men to state that he was?

Chapter Twelve

With Stephen on his way to Washington, D.C., Cassie cleaned up their breakfast dishes, then decided to walk over to Tim and Lisa's camp site. She found them eating breakfast at the picnic table. Lisa invited Cassie to join them for a cup of hot chocolate.

After chatting for a while, they decided to check with Matt to see if they could do more research in the ranger station today. They secured their campsites and headed for the station. Matt was just getting back from his rounds when they arrived.

Matt invited them inside and agreed to their request to use the station. He offered them seats at the rectangular table in the center of the room while he brought out some of the artifacts they would need for the day. Then he placed an armload books on the table, adding, "At the Park Service library, I found some books and information about coded messages used during the Civil War. What makes it tough is that there were several different ways to encrypt or to decode a message. I'm not sure if I found anything that can be used to decode the message you found."

Lisa offered, "Maybe if we knew how to use that brass cipher, we might be able to crack the code in this message." In response, Matt showed them a particular volume he'd found containing instructions on how to use a brass cipher.

Matt left the trio and went to attack the paperwork on his desk. Cassie began to read aloud from the book on ciphers,

"The soldiers assigned to signal corps used flags to relay information to each other during battle. Information regarding the enemy's movements was sent to headquarters using a coded written message. A cipher was used to encode the message by changing letters into numbers. When the message was received at headquarters, they used the same type of cipher to decode it, changing the numbers back into letters.

The outer ring of the cipher had numbers that corresponded to standard signal flag movements used by the signal corps during battle. The inner ring was stamped with the letters of the alphabet. Before a battle the signal corps was provided with the code -- number 1 equals letter X, or whatever the letter was that day."

With the others watching, Tim looked at the message and moved the outer ring of the cipher to several possible locations on the inner ring. After a few minutes of trial and error, Tim said, "We're missing something vital in the decoding process, and I believe it's the prearranged setting. The prearranged setting could be a multitude of possibilities. Also, based on what we know by the soldier's remains and other artifacts, it's highly unlikely that he was looking at signal flags during a battle. Maybe the brass cipher was not used in coding this message."

Cassie spoke up and said, "Yesterday afternoon, I was reading on line about an encryption system that was used by the Signal Corps during the Civil War. It was known as the Route Transportation Cipher. It did not require the use of a brass cipher for decoding."

Cassie turned on her laptop and found the webpage she'd bookmarked the previous day. She cleared her throat, then began reading the instructions on how to use the Route Transportation Cipher. "The first word in the message is usually a key word indicating the number of columns necessary to decipher the message and in which order the message should be read."

"How do you determine the number of columns?" asked Lisa.

Cassie responded, "You count the number of letters in the key word to determine the number of columns needed." Cassie pointed to the example in the laptop screen, "See, here's the first word or key word -- it has six letters. Then the second word of the coded message is placed into the first column, the third word is placed into the second column, and so forth. After putting the word into the sixth column, you go back to the first column and insert the next word from the message. After the message has been completely filled into the columns, then the first letter of the key word is placed on top of the first column, the second letter is placed on top of the second column, and the remaining letters of the key word are placed on top of their corresponding columns."

"This is incredible!" exclaimed Lisa.

"Now, we have to look at the letters in the key word and determine which letter comes first in the alphabet. That column with that letter is the beginning of the real message. The words in that column are read from bottom to top to reveal the message." Cassie explained.

"Then what's the next step?" asked Tim.

Cassie responded, "Now find the letter in the key word that comes next in the alphabet and read its column from the top down."

"I think I've got it," said Tim. "Then you go to the next letter in the alphabet in the key word and read that column from the bottom to the top. How clever! Let's try it on message we found in the rifle!"

They looked at the message Tim had found inside the rifle compartment:

LUNDY hollow the stored hemlock RIVERS five bricks they in THREE miles in bricks Spring to due the small Creek transported west bottom into Ivy and of of silver below kegs SEAPORT gunpowder and cave with COW-CATCHER kegs gold to loaded and Saturday melting COWCATCHER be other wagon soldiers followed will LUNDY

Matt shook his head, "It still doesn't make any sense."

Cassie replied, "According to the instructions. We just have to find the key word to help us decipher the message."

Tim grinned, "It's got to be the first word, like the instructions said -- LUNDY is the key word! Since there are five letters in the word LUNDY, we need to put the message into five columns."

Going to the whiteboard Matt had set up earlier, Cassie started to put the message into five columns. She left out LUNDY and started with the second word in the message.

hollow	the	stored	hemlock	RIVERS
five	bricks	they	in	THREE
miles	in	bricks	Spring	to
due	the	small	Creek	transported
west	bottom	into	Ivy	and
of	of	silver	below	kegs
SEAPORT	gunpowder	and	cave	with
COWCATCHER	kegs	gold	to	loaded
and	Saturday	melting	COWCATCHER	be
other	wagon	soldiers	followed	will

Everyone looked at the gridded message. Matt quizzed, "What's the next step in solving this puzzle?"

Tim explained, "According to the instructions Cassie read, the key word is LUNDY. First, we put the name at the top of the chart with L over the first column, U over the second column, and so forth."

L	U	N	D	Y
hollow	the	stored	hemlock	RIVERS
five	bricks	they	in	THREE
miles	in	bricks	Spring	to
due	the	small	Creek	transported
west	bottom	into	Ivy	and
of	of	silver	below	kegs
SEAPORT	gunpowder	and	cave	with
COWCATCHER	kegs	gold	to	loaded
and	Saturday	melting	COWCATCHER	be
other	wagon	soldiers	followed	will

If we look at the letters in LUNDY, we see that D would come first in the alphabet. So if we look at the column under the D, we start reading the message from the bottom to the top of the column.

Matt said, "Okay, that column says—Followed COW-CATCHER to cave below Ivy Creek spring in hemlock."

Lisa exclaimed, "Now that makes more sense! What's next?"

Tim continued, "The next letter in LUNDY that comes sequentially in the alphabet is L. We need to read the column under L from the top down and add it to the first portion of the message."

Matt read down the column, "hollow five miles due west of SEAPORT COWCATCHER and other."

Lisa jumped in excitedly, "I think we've got it! Now we need to read the rest of the columns in order." Cassie wrote down the message on the whiteboard as Matt read it aloud.

followed COWCATCHER to cave below Ivy Creek Spring in hemlock hollow five miles due west of SEAPORT COWCATCHER and other soldiers melting gold and silver into small bricks they stored the bricks in the bottom of gunpowder kegs Saturday wagon will be loaded with kegs and transported to THREE RIVERS

"Oh my!" exclaimed Lisa softly. "What did that soldier stumble upon?"

Cassie looked at her laptop again, "Sometimes code words are used instead of a person's real name or geographical location in many encrypted messages."

She looked at the whiteboard and declared, "It looks like we have three instances where some words have all their letters capitalized -- COWCATCHER, SEAPORT, and THREE RIVERS. These are probably code words, but for what?"

"A thought just occurred to me," said Matt as he went over to the book shelf to pull down a large atlas with detailed maps of the Shenandoah National Park. He opened to the page with Ivy Creek Spring marked on the map and looked at the scale at the bottom of the page. Matt took out a ruler and measured out 5 miles due west of Ivy Creek Spring. "It looks like SEAPORT could very well be Port Republic, Virginia!"

"Excellent, Matt!" exclaimed Tim. "Now if we can just figure out who or what COWCATCHER is and where THREE RIVERS is located, we'll have a better picture of what the message was meant to convey."

Lisa looked at group and said, "It seems that every time we answer one question, two or three more crop up!"

They continued sharing ideas and possibilities as to what

COWCATCHER and THREE RIVERS might mean. Suddenly, Cassie's eyes widened, "I grew up near Pittsburgh, Pennsylvania. Back then, there was a football stadium where the Monongahela, Youghiogheny, and Ohio Rivers converged. It was known as Three Rivers Stadium. Maybe that's the destination the soldier meant by THREE RIVERS!"

"Could very well be," said Tim as he rubbed his chin. "We now have good possibilities for what two of the capitalized words might mean. Now we need to figure out the meaning or identity of COWCATCHER."

"What is a cowcatcher, Tim?" asked Lisa.

Tim answered, "A cowcatcher is the bottom front portion of trains, especially steam locomotives, that protrudes over the railroad tracks and pushes objects off the tracks."

"So do you think COWCATCHER may have something to do with trains or steam locomotives?"

Tim paused and proposed the following, "Since the cowcatcher is part of a locomotive that the engineer operates, maybe COWCATCHER refers to an engineer. In this instance, the Union Army had engineers responsible for designing and building bridges, roads, harbors, and buildings. This may be a possibility, but until we have more information, it's just conjecture."

At that time, Cassie's cell phone rang. Recognizing Stephen's ring tone, she turned aside, "Hi, you heading back yet?"

"Cassie, you won't believe what I found at the Archives! I think I have enough evidence to prove that the remains of the soldier we found is actually Private Edward Lundawick Doherty. Odd thing though, according to the documents I found, it seems that Doherty was a traitor to his country."

Cassie quickly responded, "That can't be! From what we

found, it looks like Doherty uncovered some sort of plot to smuggle gold and silver."

"You're kidding! Finding the true story about what happened to our soldier is not as simple as we thought it would be, is it? Well, I'm on my way and should be there within the hour. Love you!"

Smiling, Cassie turned back to the group and let them know Stephen would be back soon. Being at a good stopping point for the day, the trio thanked Matt and headed back to their campsite.

At dusk, Daniel, Joy, and JD returned from their trip to Blacksburg. While they unpacked their gear, Tim got a good fire started, and Cassie and Lisa worked to prepare a quick meal of hot dogs and baked beans. Just as JD was ready to recount their experiences at Virginia Tech, Stephen drove up to the campsite. Cassie went to greet him with a hug, "Just in time for supper and stories!"

Chapter Thirteen

Just after dawn, Stephen woke the sound of several song birds calling to each other. He threw aside his covers and got up to dress. Once outside his tent, he saw Tim smiling and waving to Matt who was heading back to the ranger station. Tim walked over to Stephen and quietly said, "Matt's invited all of us to share coffee, juice, and donuts with him at the ranger station as soon as we can get over there."

"That's very nice of him," replied Stephen.

Tim responded, "Yes, it is. JD, Joy, and Daniel have already been up for an hour. They're setting up the room so we can share the information we've found so far."

"And I thought I was an early riser!" chuckled Stephen.

Stephen woke Cassie while Tim woke Lisa. The ladies freshened and dressed quickly, then walked with Stephen and Tim to the ranger station.

Matt was leaning against the rail of the front porch when he spotted them and waved a greeting. When they reached the porch, he motioned them inside to join the others. On one side of the room, the chairs were arranged in auditorium fashion facing a large projector screen and a podium. On the other side of the room was a table with a delectable selection of donuts, juice, and coffee.

After greeting each other, the group lined up and picked what they wanted to eat and drink. Once everyone had eaten and settled in their chairs, Matt invited Daniel to lead the group discussion.

Daniel stood quietly for a moment, then began, "It looks like we've gathered a wealth of information. As with any good research, questions are answered and new questions raised. I propose that we each share what we've found so far. Afterward, we'll discuss how to proceed with our project."

Everyone nodded their heads in agreement. Daniel called Stephen forward to share what he found at the National Archives. Stephen walked to the front and placed his folder of documents on the podium.

"I think we can eliminate the possibility that Private Elias L. Dixon is the person we found in the hollow. From his service and pension records, it seems that Private Dixon survived the war and went back to his home near Harrisburg, Pennsylvania, where he lived until he died in the late 1890s.

However, when I reviewed the service and pension records of Private Edward Lundawick Doherty, I found that he enlisted in the 20th Michigan Infantry in 1862 from Jackson, Michigan. Because of his excellent marksmanship skills, Private Doherty was transferred to the 1st U.S. Sharpshooters, also known as Berdan's Sharpshooters. He participated in several small skirmishes in addition to Gettysburg, where he received a commendation for using his marksmanship skills to solely render one battery ineffective.

Wanting to use his skills as a telegrapher, Private Doherty requested a transfer to the U.S. Signal Corps. From his records, it seems that he was a model soldier, the type you like to read about in novels. According to his service record, he was killed in late 1864 in the Shenandoah Valley."

Cassie smiled broadly, "Now we know who our soldier is!"

"Wait a minute, Cassie. There's more to the story. It seems

that when his wife, Mary, applied for a widow's pension, she was declined by the U.S. Government because of letters written by Lieutenant Lucius Purdy of the U.S. Engineers, a sergeant, and a corporal."

Immediately, Tim quietly queried, "Cowcatcher?!"

Stephen pulled out a photocopied document from his folder and read its contents, "I, Lieutenant Lucius Purdy, U.S. Engineers, was given the assignment to repair telegraph lines destroyed by the enemy in the Shenandoah Valley. On the afternoon of September 24, 1864, from a distance, I witnessed Sergeant Samuel Willis and Private Edward Doherty exchange documents with a Confederate officer. What I witnessed was enough to convince me that Sergeant Willis and Private Doherty were traitors to the Union Army and the United States.

My patrol and I watched both men mount their horses and ride due north into the woods. After following them for several miles, I ordered my patrol to split into two groups. Once we flanked them. I ordered Willis and Doherty to halt and surrender, but they turned their horses to escape. I gave the order to my patrol to fire their rifles. Sergeant Willis was hit, and he slumped in his saddle. Doherty yelled at Sergeant Willis to escape. Sergeant Willis continued riding his horse toward the south.

Then Doherty dismounted and commenced firing on his fellow Union soldiers. He seriously wounded three of my men before my patrol was successful in stopping him with several well-aimed rifle shots. Afterward, I gave the command for my patrol to tend the wounded and bring them back to camp. Upon our return, I searched for Sergeant Willis and could not find him. I assume he died of his wounds somewhere else.

We left Private Doherty's body to lie in disgrace in the hollow where he turned on his own fellow soldiers. Such is the fate of all traitors to the Union Army and the United States."

After Stephen read the letter, he added, "There are two more letters written by Sergeant B. Carmichael and Corporal Amos Devereaux. Their letters read the same way as Lieutenant Purdy's letter." Stephen paused before sitting down, "It's hard to believe that such a model soldier could be a traitor to the United States."

Tim then took the floor, "Lisa, Cassie, Matt, and I worked on the coded message found inside the butt of the rifle. Using references from the National Park Service and the internet, we were able to crack the code. The decoded message reads,"

"Followed COWCATCHER to cave below Ivy Creek Spring in hemlock hollow five miles due west of SEAPORT. COWCATCHER and other soldiers melting gold and silver into small bricks. They stored the bricks in the bottom of gunpowder kegs. Saturday wagon will be loaded with kegs and transported to THREE RIVERS."

Tim continued, "In this message, there are four words in all capital letters that stand out—COWCATCHER, SEAPORT, and THREE RIVERS. From what we were able to deduce, SEAPORT could be Port Republic, Virginia. Cassie shared with us yesterday that Pittsburgh, Pennsylvania, is often referred to as THREE RIVERS. Also, we were thinking that since a cowcatcher is part of a steam locomotive and that an engineer runs the locomotive, it may be that COWCATCHER was an engineer. With what Stephen shared, I wonder if COWCATCHER could possibly be Lieutenant Lucius Purdy." queried Tim as he reclaimed his seat next to Lisa.

At this point, JD began to hook up his laptop to a computer projector aimed at the large screen. Daniel took the podium and began to explain the process of computerized facial reconstruction. Daniel then asked JD to turn on the computer and bring up the file with the images they'd produced the previous day.

As the first image was shown on the screen, Daniel stated, "The first image is a reconstructed bust of the man with no hair on his head nor any facial hair, such as a mustache or eyebrows. The next image is a man with a full head of hair very typical of the Civil War time period. With a click of the mouse, JD will add a mustache to the man, then a beard. This way, we can look at several possibilities of what the man may have looked like when he was alive."

"Next, we looked at the rest of the remains. We measured the skeletal structure and downloaded the measurements into a program that enabled us to develop a full-body image of what the soldier may have looked like when he was alive."

At that point, JD clicked another button, and the full-body image appeared on the screen. With another click, JD clothed the image with a Union Army uniform. As JD rotated the image on screen, everyone was amazed at how real the 3-D image of the soldier looked.

Lisa declared, "Now we now have an idea of how the soldier looked in real life and his history of service in the army. This is simply amazing! What more do can we do to complete the story of Private Doherty?"

"That's a good question, Lisa. We'll need to think outside the box now," said Stephen.

"What do you mean?" asked Lisa.

Stephen replied, "Well, we should take some time to examine the gunpowder kegs found inside the cave to see if they could possibly be the ones mentioned in the note."

"What else?" asked Cassie.

Tim interjected, "We also need to find more background information concerning Private Doherty."

"We can try to find any direct descendants of Private Doherty and interview them to find more possible information about him," offered Cassie.

After more discussion, Daniel, JD, and Joy decided they would explore the cave again. Stephen, Cassie, Tim, and Lisa took on the assignment of finding direct descendants of Private Doherty.

Chapter Fourteen

The morning was already hot and humid when JD and Daniel met Joy near the trail head by the campground store. They were outfitted with well-equipped backpacks to help them explore the cave. After walking down the trail for about half an hour, they arrived at the Ivy Creek Spring shelter. Sweating profusely, JD filled his canteen with the cold spring water and splashed the refreshing water on his face.

After savoring the cool spring water and relaxing a few minutes in the shade, the three hiked the rest of the way to the cave in the hemlock hollow. They removed the rocks and branches from the entrance and entered the cave. Turning on their flashlights to illuminate the cavern, they saw the small gunpowder kegs against a side wall. JD selected one keg and began to pry the boards from the top while Joy provided the light. Inside they saw nothing but gunpowder, just like before.

"I thought for sure we'd find gold or silver in the keg," said Joy disappointedly.

Daniel responded, "I've got an idea. Hold your light above the keg. JD, let's scoop out the gunpowder and see if there's anything at the bottom."

While Joy held her flashlight above the keg, JD and Daniel scooped out the powder onto the ground. When they got halfway down the keg, they struck more wooden planks. With a small digging trowel and JD's multi-purpose knife, Daniel pried the planks loose and removed them. Joy tilted her light to shine inside the keg. They were surprised to see the light reflecting back at them.

Daniel reached in and pulled out a beautifully handcrafted chalice. "Wow!" exclaimed Joy, "And there's more in there!" Daniel told Joy to hold both her light and his on the chalice. "This will take more light then our flashlights," he said. "Let's get the LED lanterns our of our packs.

With the cavern now well lit, they set to work. As Daniel pulled each piece out of the keg, he held them for JD to photograph. There were several religious artifacts in the keg—the chalice, a crucifix, and an incense burner with a gold-link chain attached. After JD was done, he placed them together as one group on the dirt floor next to the cavern wall.

Joy exclaimed, "I can't begin to imagine the value of each piece. With the value of gold today, I'm guessing that what we see here may be worth quite a bit!"

"Let's take a look in the other kegs and see what else we can find," said Daniel.

Daniel and JD went to the next keg and repeated the process of removing the gunpowder and false bottom, photographing each find, and grouping the items against the wall.

When they opened the sixth keg, Joy shined her light inside. Daniel whistled softly and said, "Can you believe this?!" He pulled out the first of six small ingots of gold and silver.

They meticulously finished the process with the remaining six kegs. Most of the kegs contained a stash of religious icons made of gold or silver. However, in the last keg, they found a leather bag containing small diamonds, emeralds, rubies, plain gold wedding bands, and one larger signet ring. JD immediately recognized the symbols on the signet ring. "This is significant—I think we had better show this ring to the others as soon as we get back to camp," he declared.

With their tasks completed, they sat down on nearby boulders and quietly sipped the cool spring mountain water from their canteens.

JD broke the silence by angrily asking, "What kind of men would break into churches and steal their religious icons?"

Daniel shook his head and said, "I honestly don't know, but it's apparent that these men must have pillaged quite a few churches and other places. I'm willing to bet that Private Doherty must have found out about it, hence the coded note. Let's continue searching this cave; we might find something else."

"There's something that seems odd..." Joy said thoughtfully.

"What's that?" asked JD.

Joy asked, "Remember what the coded message said—that everything had been melted down?"

"Yeah?"

Joy pointed out, "Notice that we only found a few ingots of gold in one keg?"

Daniel jumped into the conversation, "Yeah, you're right! They'd probably just started the process of smelting this load of artifacts into ingots, but something stopped them. I know they were interrupted by Willis and Doherty, but they were killed and no longer a problem."

"But something kept these guys from coming back to finish the job," interjected JD, "Otherwise..."

"All this stuff would have been melted into ingots and gone. Something else interrupted them, but what?" asked Joy.

JD shook his head and chuckled, "Another mystery!"

After their break, the trio began searching other areas of the cave. Daniel scanned the cave floor with his metal detector for any other metal objects. Three times the indicator beeped letting him know there was metal in the dirt. Each time, Joy knelt to uncover what appeared to be some vintage minié balls, exposing them for JD to photograph.

As they continued toward the dead-end portion of the cave, the metal detector emitted a slightly different signal. Joy knelt down and started digging one more time. She dug up a very small brass disk with a hole near the edge and handed it to JD with a shrug. Using his shirt tail, he cleaned the dirt from the disk, exposing the etched words—Lt. Lucius Purdy. He showed it to the others.

"What do you think? A dog tag?" asked JD.

"Sure looks like one," replied Daniel.

Now they had something to tie Lieutenant Lucius Purdy to the cave! Excited about all they'd discovered, the trio decided it was time to head back to the campground.

JD looked around the cave thoughtfully, "What do we do with all of this stuff? It's not smart to just leave it here."

Joy replied, "We're going to have to get it all out of here to the ranger station and report our findings to Park Service. JD, why don't you and I take a load back and get the others to help carry the rest of the artifacts out? Do you mind staying here to stand guard, Daniel?"

Daniel agreed, "Sure, no problem. I'll do a few more sweeps with my detector while you're gone."

They wrapped several of the artifacts and carefully placed them into their backpacks. Once the packs were ready, JD and Joy started hiking back to the ranger station, leaving Daniel behind at the cave entrance.

Chapter Fifteen

While JD, Joy, and Daniel were exploring the cave, Cassie and Lisa took on the challenge of doing internet searches for census information pertaining to Private Edward L. Doherty. Lisa offered, "Cassie, I have a paid subscription to a genealogical research website. We should be able to do census searches without any problem."

Lisa sat at her laptop and brought up the genealogical site. "We know that Edward L. Doherty came from Jackson, Michigan. Let's see which county that is since that's how census records are sectioned." Using her on-line search engine, Lisa declared, "Looks it's in Jackson County, Michigan."

With that new piece of information, Lisa began searching her genealogical site for the 1860 census records of Jackson County, Michigan. Census records were not indexed, but set up with by family head of household on each street or road. Lisa and Cassie patiently scrolled through screen after screen of handwritten records, concentrating on the name Doherty. At times they struggled with deciphering the census taker's handwriting on some records, but within a few minutes, they found a Doherty family living in Jackson, Michigan. The head of the household was Samuel Doherty and his wife's name was Eleanor. He was a shop owner and a telegrapher. However, Edward L. Doherty was not listed with them.

"I thought for sure that we had found Edward and his family," Cassie said disappointedly.

Lisa scrolled one more page and exclaimed, "Here he is! This record is for a different house—a judge and his family. It lists Edward L. Doherty as a boarder and a law clerk for the judge. He was born in Michigan and was 25 years old at the time of this census. It's possible his actual family was the record on the previous page."

"Look here, Cassie! The judge had an 18-year-old daughter named Mary. Maybe she's the young woman in the daguerreotype you found." Lisa said excitedly.

"Wow! Let's save this record to your laptop, then see if we can find anything about the Doherty's in Jackson County in 1870 census records," said Cassie.

Lisa downloaded the 1860 record into a Doherty folder she created on her desktop. Then she pulled up the 1870 census records for Jackson County. They scrolled through each page of the records, but could not find a listing for Mary Doherty.

Cassie looked at Lisa, "This doesn't make sense, we should have found her if she had married Edward. Unless... they moved away after they were married! Is there any other type of record we can look at that would help us?"

"Well, let's see... there's another genealogical site I use when I do family research where people post their family trees. It's possible someone has already done research on the Doherty line and has posted it. Let's see what we can find there."

In a few moments, Lisa pulled up the website and entered the search query for Edward L. Doherty living in Jackson, Michigan. A record appeared listing Edward L. Doherty as the first-born son of Samuel and Eleanor Doherty. There was a side note on the record. It showed that Samuel Doherty was a Mason and was one of the first in Jackson County to learn Morse code. He owned a hardware store in downtown Jackson, specializing in selling wire and other supplies dealing with telegraphy.

Lisa electronically copied the record and filed it in the laptop's Doherty file. As she continued the search, Lisa found an 1861 family tree record listing Edward L. as the head of the household, with a wife named Mary and a son named John Samuel Doherty. The record showed that Edward died in 1864, but did not mention his military record. However, when Lisa tagged Mary's name, it showed some surprising information.

"Look here, Cassie. Mary Doherty died in Ramona, Washington County, Oklahoma, in 1911! That's strange—people usually stayed in one location back then. Wonder why she left Michigan to go to Oklahoma?"

"Now at least we know the next place to search! I thought we'd reached a dead end when neither Edward L. nor Mary were listed in the 1870 census, but now we can look at the 1910 census records for Washington County, Oklahoma," said Cassie.

Lisa switched back to the census records website. This time, she pulled up the 1910 census records for Washington County, Oklahoma. She scrolled through each page until she came to the pages referring to Ramona, Oklahoma. She and Cassie methodically scanned each line for Mary Doherty. They spied her name at the same time.

Mary was living with the family of J.S. Doherty. J.S. Doherty was listed as a 39-year-old male, born in Michigan. Among his family members was Mary, who was listed as a 58-year-old widow, born in Michigan. He worked as a laborer in the oil fields. After reviewing the information, Lisa saved it to her laptop's Doherty file.

With that encouraging find, Cassie and Lisa searched the Oklahoma census records of 1920 through 1940. Once they got to the 1940 census, they found only one Doherty family still present in Ramona, Oklahoma–Roy (son of J.S. Doherty) and

Stella Doherty and their 3-year-old son—James Doherty.

"I wonder if James Doherty is still alive and living in Ramona?" asked Lisa. She keyed in another search on her web browser and found the address and phone number of James L. Doherty in Ramona, Oklahoma. Cassie wrote down the name and number, "Let's see if we can get Tim or Stephen to call him!"

Chapter Sixteen

While Cassie and Lisa were doing their research, Tim and Stephen decided to search on line for historical information about missing gold and silver in the Shenandoah Valley near the Winchester and Front Royal area. As they sat down to access Tim's laptop, Stephen wondered, "So the coded note said that gold and silver were stolen, but from where and when? Boy, talk about trying to find a needle in a haystack!"

"We'll have to narrow down the possibilities. A Boolean search should do it," replied Tim.

Stephen responded, "Yep! That's a start, but we're going to have to be creative in determining what word combinations will work."

"Okay, so what do you recommend, partner?"

"Let's try 'Civil War' and 'gold and silver theft'."

When Tim typed in the Boolean search combination, several dozen web pages came up on the laptop screen. Each webpage was opened and read, but nothing stood out as a definite possibility. Next Stephen recommended, "Try 'gold and silver' and 'theft' and 'Shenandoah Valley' and 'Civil War'."

Tim typed in the string of words and pulled up several more web pages. As they reviewed each web page, there was one report written by a member of Imboden's command from the Confederate army.

"Take a look at this, Stephen!"

Stephen looked over Tim's shoulder and started reading, 'While on patrol with my command in the Shenandoah Valley, I saw a large plume of smoke coming from the direction of Nortonsville. Not hearing any artillery or rifle fire, I led my patrol to investigate.

When we arrived, we saw that the Methodist church had been set on fire. A crying woman ran up, pleading with us to help her husband, the minister of the church. Her husband was lying badly beaten near the fence in the church yard.

While we tended to his wounds, the minister's wife told us earlier that morning, a band of Yankee soldiers on horseback had arrived at the church and demanded to see the minister. Her husband met with them, asking how he could help. The officer demanded that her husband surrender all the gold and silver inside the church building.

When her husband tried to reason with him, the officer ordered his men to bind the minister's feet together and to hang him upside down from a tree. The wife saw what was happening and ran out of their house, pleading with the Yankee officer to release her husband. The officer laughed and told her that she had a choice -- he could hang either by his feet or his neck. She ran to her husband to provide what comfort she could.

Then the officer shouted orders to his men to ransack the church. They came out with a gold chalice, a silver plate, and a gold cross. The officer became angry with what little they'd found inside and ordered some of his men to burn down the church. While waiting, several other soldiers punched her husband in the face and spat upon him. The officer then ordered his men to mount their horses, and they rode away.

After hearing her story, I ordered my patrol to search the surrounding area for the Yankee thieves. Two of my men stayed behind to help the minister and his wife. As we searched the area, several citizens reported they had seen the Yankees riding due east toward the Union Army encampment. We continued our search, but were unsuccessful in finding them.

Captain Solomon Armstrong, 62nd Partisan Rangers'

Stephen looked up and said to Tim, "Could this be a link to our soldier?"

"Let's bookmark it so we can refer to it later," said Tim.

Lisa walked over to where they were working and excitedly interrupted them, "We think we found a descendant of Edward Doherty in Ramona, Oklahoma. We have his phone number, but Cassie and I thought it might be better if a guy called him instead of one of us. Tim, would you mind making a phone call to Mr. Doherty?"

"No, I don't mind at all," smiled Tim.

Chapter Seventeen

Lisa gave Tim the phone number, and he dialed it on his cell phone, placing it on speaker so the group could hear. After three rings, a voice replied, "Hello, Jim Doherty speakin'."

"Mr. Doherty, my name is Tim Gentry. I'm working with a group doing genealogical research on Mary Doherty and her son, John Samuel Doherty. Are their names familiar to you?"

"Why do you want to know? What's this all about?"

"We're looking for descendants of Mary Doherty to see if we can find more information. From what we've been able to discover, Mary Doherty and her son, John Samuel Doherty, moved from Jackson, Michigan, to Ramona, Oklahoma, several years after the Civil War. We were wondering if you are related in some way to Mary and her son, John Samuel Doherty?"

There was a long pause at the other end of the phone. Tim was about to ask if he was still on the line when Jim Doherty spoke, "Yes, I'm the grandson of John Samuel Doherty. I never knew his mother, Mary Doherty. I seem to remember that my dad said they both came from some place in Michigan. She died in 1911, and my grandfather died a few years later. Both of them are buried in a local cemetery here. Why are you all so interested in Mary Doherty?"

Tim explained, "We found a daguerreotype of a young woman. Inside, there was a note that said, 'LUNDY, with all my love. Mary'. We think it may have been a gift given by Mary to her husband, Edward L. Doherty. Since it appears that Mary and Edward L. are your ancestors, would you like to have a copy of the photo?"

"Yes, I would. I do have photographs of her here in Ramona as an old woman. I don't have any photos of her when she was younger."

"Do you have a computer, Mr. Doherty?" asked Tim.

"No, but my grandson has one. He lives next door to my wife and me."

"Well, Mr. Doherty, if you check with your grandson and get his e-mail address, we'll scan the daguerreotype and e-mail a copy to you. I'll give you my phone number so you can call me back after you speak to your grandson."

"That's right nice of y'all! Appreciate that a lot!"

"Our pleasure, Sir!"

Once the conversation was completed, Lisa and Cassie scanned the daguerreotype into file that could be e-mailed to Mr. Doherty. Within an hour, Tim received a return call from Jim Doherty. Tim e-mailed the file and asked if it had been received. Doherty replied, "Thank you! I definitely can see the similarities between the younger Mary and the photos of Mary when she was in her seventies. This sure means a lot to me!"

"Y'know, when I saw that picture, I couldn't help but think there was something very familiar about it and then it dawned on me. What was familiar to me was the frame. Several years ago, my grandfather gave me a small picture in a pewter frame with two small loops of metal on its right side. In fact, before I called, I pulled it out and compared it to the frame in the picture you sent me -- the frames matched! The photo in my pewter frame is of a young man dressed in a dark jacket and a check- ered shirt. I was told by my grandfather that the young man was his father. Would you all like a copy of this picture?"

Tim replied, "Yes, thank you!"

"You're quite welcome," Jim responded. "You know, I think y'all might be interested in something else that my grandfather gave me when I was a young boy."

"What's that?" asked Tim.

"It's a small journal my great-grandfather wrote that was mailed to his wife sometime after he died. It's interesting readin', but what has puzzled the family for years is the instruction at the end of the story. Part of it is washed out and smeared so you can't read it."

"What does the end say?"

"It says, 'Find Sergeant Samuel Willis, U.S. Signal Corps. He will tel—'. We can't read anything after that, but we sure are curious about it," Jim stated.

Tim offered, "Well, we do have a little bit of information about a Sergeant Willis. Would you be able to scan and e-mail a copy of the letter to us? We are definitely interested in reading it and can work on trying to figure out the last instruction."

"I'll have my grandson scan the pages and get it to y'all." There was a brief pause, then Jim Doherty spoke again, "I just have a gut feelin' this is the right thing to do. Somehow, I can't help but feel God's Hand in all of this. Thank y'all so much for your help!"

"Glad to do it, sir! We'll contact you as soon as we find out more information."

After the call ended, Tim turned to the others and smiled, "I have to agree with Mr. Doherty—God's Hand must be in all of this."

Chapter Eighteen

Later that afternoon, JD and Joy arrived at the ranger station.

"You'll never guess what we found!" JD exclaimed.

Cassie laughed, "Okay, I give up. What'd you find?"

"You'll see! First, help us empty our backpacks onto a table."

Tim and Stephen removed the laptop from the table and helped Joy and JD take off their backpacks.

"Whoa! These packs are heavy! What do you have in them, rocks?!"

"Something a little more valuable than rocks!"

As they emptied the backpacks, Cassie and Lisa began to unwrap each item. The first item Cassie unwrapped was an ornate gold crucifix. She held it tenderly and remarked, "This crucifix reminds me of St. Martha's where I used to worship as a little girl in Pennsylvania."

Stephen gingerly unwrapped the next item, a silver plate with an inscription engraved on the bottom. After reading it, he held out the plate, "Hey Tim! Take a look at this!"

Tim took the plate and tilted it toward the window so he could see the inscription more clearly in the sunlight—First Methodist Church, Nortonsville, Virginia 1843. "Well, I'll be! This is incredible! We were just reading about this church on the Web!"

JD asked, "What are you guys talking about?"

Stephen responded, "Earlier this afternoon, Tim and I did

some on-line searches and found a report detailing the robbery of this particular church!"

"That seems to fit. The rest of these are items you'd normally find in a place of worship," replied JD.

Joy reached into her backpack and pulled out a ring and gave it to Stephen. When Stephen saw it, his jaw dropped open, "My word! This is a Masonic ring!"

Immediately, everyone stopped what they were doing to take turns looking at the ring. Tim examined it, saying to the others, "Did you notice the inside of the ring? It's engraved with the initials, E.L.D."

"Those are the initials of our soldier!" exclaimed Cassie.

Lisa added, "It's got to be Lundy's ring!"

Tears pricked Cassie's eyes as she said what everyone in the room was thinking, "They killed him and stole his ring."

Tim directed their thoughts back to the present, "Folks, let's continue. Joy, did you find anything else in the cave?"

Joy said, "Yes, there's a lot more just like it back at the cave —each barrel had a false bottom where the items we hidden. Daniel stayed behind to keep guard, but we need get right back so we can bring everything up to the ranger station before it gets dark."

Stephen spoke up, "Tim and I will go back with you. Matt, do you have any more space in your secure area?"

Matt replied, "Sure. There's a small storage room with shelves in the back, and the whole room can be locked."

Cassie and Lisa volunteered to stay and inventory the items and place them on the storage room shelves. Stephen, JD, and Tim shouldered their backpacks, now filled with wrapping materials, and followed Joy back down the trail.

Alerting Daniel to their arrival, they entered the cave. Soon everyone was carefully wrapping and packing the remaining artifacts into their backpacks. By the time the job was done, the afternoon sun was just above the horizon. They slung their backpacks over their shoulders and started hiking back to the ranger station.

As they walked up the trail, the sky displayed wondrous shades of red, violet, and orange. For fun, Tim called out some of the cadences he'd learned in the army. Soon each hiker was taking a turn leading the chant. The group arrived at the ranger station just as dusk was beginning to settle into the campground. The weary hikers went inside and placed their backpacks on the floor by the table.

Everyone worked together to process every item from the cave. Stephen and Tim handed items from the backpacks to Joy and JD for unwrapping. Items were then handed to Daniel and Lisa to inventory into their laptops, then Cassie took the items and placed them on the storage room shelves.

They finished just as Matt returned from his rounds of the campground. Daniel and Joy showed him the items the group had stowed and watched as he secured the closet door with a padlock. As the trio returned to the main room, Matt used his keys to lock the storage room behind them.

They joined the group in time to hear Cassie say, "While Lisa and I were back in the storage room, we saw several more engraved markings and names on the artifacts that might be helpful in identifying their rightful owners.

"That sounds like something we can start on tomorrow morning," said Daniel. "We've had a long day already."

JD added, "And I'm getting hungry!"

Everyone laughed and realized it was time to shut down the research project for the night. Joy called Park Service and submitted her report about their activities for the day. Ushering the group out, Matt locked the station door for the night.

After eating a quick supper of hotdogs roasted over the campfire, the weary bunch dispersed to their tents. It wasn't long before the cool night air and the sound of a rustling breeze rippling through the leaves of the surrounding trees lulled each one to a restful, well-earned sleep.

Chapter Nineteen

The following morning greeted them with sparkling dew on every item left outside their tents. White tail does and spotted fawns grazed nearby, taking advantage of the quiet morning before all the campers rose for the day.

After a hearty breakfast, the group walked together to the ranger station to begin another day of research and discovery. As the younger members walked swiftly ahead of their elders, Stephen smiled, "Guess I'm not as spry as I used to be. After carrying a load of gold and silver from the hollow to the ranger station, I've found I have muscles on top of muscles that I never knew I had, and every one of them is stiff and sore!" Cassie countered, "You're no spring chicken anymore!" Everyone was laughing as they entered the ranger station, bidding Matt a good morning.

While the others visited with Matt, Lisa set up her laptop and turned it on to check for e-mails from Jim Doherty. After typing in her ID and password, her site came to life. Lisa saw an e-mail from Peter Doherty, the grandson of Jim Doherty. When she opened it, there were two attachments. She clicked on the first attachment. When it opened, Lisa gasped, "Hey everyone! Take a look at this!"

On her screen was a daguerreotype of a young man in a dress shirt and jacket. The frame looked exactly like the one Cassie had found in the hemlock hollow.

"He looks just like the reconstruction we did on the computer in my lab." said Joy quietly.

"The only difference I see is that we didn't account for him having curly hair. With this, I think we can safely say that the skeletal remains belong to Edward Lundawick Doherty," replied Daniel confidently.

"I'm getting goose bumps just looking at an actual image of Lundy," said Cassie.

Lisa downloaded the photo into the Doherty file on her desktop and opened the next attachment from Peter's e-mail.

Lisa did a double-take as she viewed the screen, "When he said he'd send a small journal, I thought he'd send five or six pages, but there are a couple dozen pages here! He must have sent the journal, too."

JD began to read over her shoulder:

"To my beloved Mary,

After witnessing and being a part of many horrors and atrocities of war, I can now claim that I have peace within that only my Savior Jesus Christ can give.   A few weeks ago, Sergeant Sam Willis same by and informed me the Captain wanted to see me. He escorted me to the Captain's tent, then stuck his head inside to announce me. The Captain invited both of us to come inside.

Captain Alton Goode stood up from behind his desk, 'At ease, men. Doherty, I understand you worked as a law clerk with a judge in Jackson County, Michigan. I've also heard comments from the men that you are intelligent and quick when it comes to deciphering coded messages. From all I've heard about you, I think you have the makings of a fine officer, but I understand you've already turned down several opportunities to be promoted. I am curious, why would you turn down such an opportunity?'

I replied to Captain Goode that I appreciated his kind comments, but the reason why I chose not to become an officer was that I would find it most difficult to accept the responsibility of causing men to die because I had ordered them into battle.

The captain stood quietly for a moment, then he shared with me that he had been a pastor in New York before volunteering for the Union Army. He said he'd been approached about being an officer when others saw how many men respected him and counted on him for counsel. He originally had the same thoughts that I had about being promoted, but eventually felt God was calling him to a different leadership role.

He had great hope that in this new role, he would be able to share the Gospel and help prepare men for eternity as they faced many hardships, even death, in battle. Captain Goode continued by saying that we weren't guaranteed an easy life free from hardship and troubles, but we were guaranteed eternal life and peace in all circumstances once we placed our trust in Christ as our Savior.

I listened to him intently, somewhat surprised to have such an attitude expressed by an officer. Captain Goode concluded by encouraging me to do my duty and follow wherever God was leading during these trying times. He shook my hand and extended an invitation to come by any time if I ever wanted to know more about Christ as Savior. I thanked him and told him I would ponder everything he had shared with me.

To be quite honest, Mary, I never had anyone speak to me like that. Everyone in our camp thinks very highly of Captain Goode, and now I know why.

Sergeant Willis and I walked back toward my tent. He is an older man whose face looks like it has seen the roughest life a man could imagine, but at the same time, his eyes reveal a gentleness and kindness that drew me to him. I think you would like him, Mary.

He spoke quietly to me as we walked, 'In early summer of 1862, my brother, Jim, and I were working with our father in his blacksmith shop in Orange County, New York. One day, we heard that the town sheriff was going to speak in the town square concerning the war. Jim and I went to listen to him; he spoke about our duty as citizens to preserve the Union.

The more he spoke, the more Jim and I became convinced that he was right. At the end of his speech, the sheriff looked out over the audience and declared that he was raising a company of men to serve in 124th New York Infantry and asked for all able-bodied men to join him. Jim and I decided to enlist that day because we felt we should do our part to help save the Union.

In the months that followed, we were engaged in some skirmishes and battles. We saw men dying from wounds received in battle and many more dying from camp sicknesses. Life as a soldier was not quite the adventure we'd imagined. In fact, all Jim and I kept thinking about was how much we missed working side by side with our father in the blacksmith shop. Often, we wondered if we would ever see home again.

In the summer of 1863, our regiment received orders to move out, heading North. After marching for two days straight, we set up camp near the border of Pennsylvania. That evening, as we were finishing our meals, Captain Goode sent word around camp that he wanted to speak with all the men. My brother and I went with the rest of the company and sat on the ground around the large rock where Captain Goode was seated.

Captain Goode stood up and told us that we were going to face a very fearsome enemy determined to destroy us. He encouraged us to use the rest of the evening to prepare ourselves for what we would face tomorrow.

At the end of his talk, Captain Goode quoted the 23rd

Psalm, then asked if any man would like to come forward to pray. I was surprised when my brother stood up and went forward along with several others. As he knelt on the ground with his eyes closed and his head bowed, the Captain placed his hands on Jim's shoulders to pray for him.

In our tent later that night, Jim quietly shared that he couldn't explain why, but he felt like he needed to go forward when the Captain offered the men to come pray with him.

The next day, our regiment received orders to move up with the rest of the brigade. We dug in at Houck's Ridge near Devil's Den in Gettysburg. I will never forget that awful, fearsome fight. It seemed like we were fighting the whole rebel army. The black smoke from all the rifles and cannons was so thick we could hardly see several feet in front of us. The minié balls seemed madder than hornets and were looking to kill anything in their way.

Jim and I had dug in behind some boulders for cover. Jim stood up beside me to fire his rifle, then slumped to the ground —he had been shot in the chest! He lay on ground holding his chest and moanin', 'Momma! It hurts! Make it stop hurtin', Momma! Momma!'

I dropped my rifle and knelt down beside by brother, trying to tend to his wound while ignoring the minié balls flying by on both sides of me. As I tried to stop the bleeding, I assured him, 'It'll be all right, Jim! I'll take care of you!'

But his breathing became slower and slower. Finally, Jim opened his eyes and looked beyond me with a surprised look on his face, saying, 'Momma?! Is that you? It's me, Jim!' I looked over my shoulder to see if Momma was actually there. I couldn't see her, but somehow, Jim could see her.

I knew then he was dying and, hard as I tried, I couldn't stop him. Jim was barely breathing when I heard him excitedly whisper as he looked beyond me, 'Wait for me, Momma! I want to come with you!'. I can't explain how he knew it was her, 'cause Momma had died when Jim was just a small boy. Then he took his last breath and was gone.

I held him close as the battle raged around me, begging God over and over again to bring him back. I didn't care whether I lived or died. The reasons to fight seemed so pointless with my brother gone.

Finally, the battle was over. Captain Goode found me sitting behind the boulder cradling Jim's head in my lap. He touched my shoulder, 'Sam, help me carry Jim over yonder by that shade tree. I think he would like that spot.'

Together, we carried Jim to the tree and buried him. The Captain wrote Jim's name on a wooden plank, and I planted it at the head of his grave. Captain Goode quietly stayed with me as I stood there by the gravesite.

After a while, Captain broke the silence, saying God knew what I was going through. His only Son had been killed, too. Even though people brutally beat and hung His Son on a cross, it was part of a greater plan to demonstrate God's love for us.

Captain Goode continued to speak as we walked back to camp; I could sense there was something real and genuine about his faith in Jesus Christ as his Savior.

Within a few days, I went to Captain Goode and talked with him some more about God and His Son. He read to me from the Bible and led me in prayer so I could have Christ as my own Savior. I now know I can endure the horrors of battle, even death itself, because my Savior first endured it for me.'

I was quiet for a long while after Sergeant Willis finished talking. I thanked him for telling me his story and said I had a lot to think about. He turned to me and said, 'I have no regrets about my decision, Lundy. I just hope you will make that decision for yourself soon.'

I replied, 'I've seen many men die, and I killed men when I was a part of the 1st U.S. Sharpshooters. I didn't think about killing in the beginning, but as the days turned into months, I couldn't help but think about all those I killed in particular, one young man at Gettysburg. I try to sleep at night, but I can still see the surprised look on his face just as my rifle shot hit him. If God is so caring and so powerful, why doesn't He stop this war?!'

Sergeant Willis looked at me and replied, 'Lundy, it's not really a question of why God does or doesn't stop things from happening. I've come to realize that God gave people the right to choose whether to accept His way or not. Just like each man must choose to make God's Son his own Savior or reject Him. Some choose to follow ways opposite of what God intended, and when that happens, people suffer. According to the Bible, God's Son was brutally beaten and killed on a cross, then buried in a tomb. But three days later, He actually came back to life! He didn't just wake up, Lundy -- God used His power to raise His Son from the dead! By doing that, He showed us that He has victory over death - our biggest fear. I wanted that same victory for myself, so I chose to accept God's Son as my own Savior.

Lundy, you know that little leather pouch you carry with you all the time? I've seen you open it many times to look at a picture of your wife. After you looked at it, you put it back inside the leather pouch, then placed it inside your jacket next to your heart. Remember when you thought you'd lost it? You nearly tore the entire camp apart looking for it and said you'd pay any price to get it back. When you found it, you were so happy that you whooped and hollered and danced all around the camp. I guess what I'm trying to say is you deemed that picture a treasure, so valuable to you that you searched high and low for it until it was found. After you found it, you were exceedingly happy and put it back in that special place next to your heart.

That's what it's like with God and us. Because we're deemed so valuable to Him, He was willing to pay any price to draw us close to Him -- rejection and even the horrible death of His only Son. The Bible calls it being redeemed.

Lundy, the Bible also tells us about an enemy who wants to steal us away from knowing God's peace and destroy us before we have the chance to choose His Son as our Savior. That enemy uses things, like this war, as terrible tools to separate men from accepting what God's Son did for them on the cross.

The horrors of this war haunt us all to the point where we feel that God should reject us for all the killing we've done. It's the same tactic the enemy uses again and again, making us think we have to be good enough or clean enough before we can be deemed as a treasure by God.

But, Lundy, nothing could be further from the truth. God already made the decision that we are His treasure, and no one has the authority to change His decision. So how do we battle this enemy? What can we do? We fight the good fight -- we choose to accept that God was willing to pay the terrible price of His Son's death to redeem us. We choose to believe God when He says He treasures us and wants us close to His heart.

Lundy, it's up to you to choose to whether or not to believe God wants to redeem you as His valuable treasure.'

Tears welled up in my eyes as I pondered what Sergeant Willis was saying to me. I asked him to show me how to tell God that I choose to accept His Son's death as redemption or payment for my wrong choices and that I choose to follow His way.

Sergeant smiled and said we should pray. As we prayed, I became fully aware of my wrong choices in life. My sorrow for these choices was so strong, I thought my heart would break.

I told God how sorry I was and that I believed Him when He said He came to redeem me and that I was a valuable treasure to Him. Then I felt a strong conviction in me that I was forgiven of all I had done wrong. I couldn't help but thank Him over and over again. Mary, I have been wanting this peace for so long. That is why I am writing this to you. I want you to know that I now have the same Savior that you have!

My dearest Mary, I know not what the remaining days of this war will bring. Soon I will be going on a special mission. If you don't hear from me, find Sergeant Samuel Willis, U.S. Signal Corps. He will tel—'

"Sorry, I can't make out the rest of it," said JD.

The group was silent as they absorbed all they'd heard. Finally, Lisa reverently uttered what they all felt, "What an amazing story!"

Chapter Twenty

Joy's cell phone rang while the group was discussing the journal. Seeing it was from Park Headquarters, she stepped away from the others to take the call. When Cassie glanced that direction, she realized Joy had become distressed. She walked over, "What's wrong, Joy?"

Joy addressed the group, "That call was from Park Service —they're sending out a special truck to pick up all the gold and silver artifacts we found in the cave. I told them we'd only done a preliminary inventory and had more work to do, but they wouldn't budge. Once the items are gone, we won't have access to them to continue our research. What should we do? We only have an hour or so before they get here!"

Daniel immediately took charge, "Let's clear off the tables in this room, then start a chain to transfer the items from storage to the tables. JD, as each artifact is placed on the table, use your Tablet to take a photo, making sure to get a clear shot of any inscriptions or markings. Let's get to it, guys!"

They formed an assembly line, with Tim manning the shelves, Lisa next to him, followed by Cassie, Joy, and Stephen, then Matt at the end placing the items on the tables. Daniel worked the tables, positioning each piece so JD could get clear shots of each artifact. The group worked as quickly, but carefully, as they could. The last two items were about to be photographed when they heard knocking at the door.

Matt opened it, and there stood a Chief Park Ranger and two uniformed Park Police officers. "Good morning! We're from Park Headquarters. We have instructions to transport the some artifacts to a secure location."

Matt responded, "May I see your orders, please?"

One of the Park Police officers handed Matt a clipboard of papers. Matt scanned the documents and turned to the others, "These are legitimate orders from Headquarters." Moving to allow the men to enter, Matt added, "We need to let them do their job."

Lisa spoke up, "What will happen with all these items?"

The Chief answered, "Our people will do an intensive inventory of the artifacts and try to determine where they came from. If we're successful, we'll be able to return the artifacts to their rightful owners."

"We'll still be here a few more days, why don't you let us help by doing the research?" Lisa offered.

"With all due respect, Ma'am, we'll leave that to the appropriate professionals."

Tim spoke up with determined authority, "Sir, I believe this group represents several professional fields of expertise. Daniel has a Masters in anthropology and is contracted with Park Services, Joy is proficient using computer technology for forensic research and is also contracted by Park Services, JD is a skilled wordsmith and photographer, Stephen is trained in doing Civil War genealogical research, and..."

The Chief Park Ranger grinned and held up his hands in surrender, "Hold on! Hold on! I get the point! We would appreciate any help your group can provide. Continue your research on the artifacts, and report in daily. If you find something significant, contact us as soon as possible."

He handed Tim his business card, "Here's my contact

information. I'm looking forward to your reports!"

That being settled, the group pitched in to help the Park Headquarters men pack the artifacts for transport. When the boxes were all packed and sealed, they carried the boxes to a Park Services step van.

Shaking everyone's hand, the Chief Park Ranger said, "Thank you all for your help! Give me a call when you think you have something."

Daniel answered for all of them, "We'll do that, sir."

Chapter Twenty-One

Since it was already late morning, they decided to break for lunch. As they ate sandwiches and chips, Joy said quietly, "When I did my report last night, I no idea headquarters would send a truck to take the artifacts away."

Daniel replied, "Don't worry about it. We know you didn't make the decision to move the artifacts. And we've still got plenty of data to work with—the inventory and photos. With those, we should have enough to start researching records for owners of the artifacts. Anyone want to help me do some heavy duty browsing?" Joy and JD volunteered, then went to set up their laptops to start their on-line searching.

Daniel continued, "There are a couple more things that should to be done. I'm thinking we need to have more archival work done. This time, the service and pension records of Lieutenant Purdy and his men should be checked. Also, Joy brought up a point while we were in the cave. Only a few of the items had actually been melted down into ingots, so something critical must have interrupted their work. Stephen, do you mind going back to the National Archives to see what you can find?"

"Don't mind at all! Hey, Tim, how about coming with me?"

"Sure! I've been wanting to see how you do your Civil War research."

Daniel continued, "Great! One last thing—we need to find out any information we can about Sergeant Samuel Willis...."

Lisa excitedly responded, "Cassie and I can do that!"

"Okay, folks! We all have our assignments, so let's get to it!"

The next 24 hours would prove very interesting for all three teams.

Chapter Twenty-Two

Daniel set up his laptop next to JD and Joy, "We have JD's photos of the artifacts and the inventory notes made yesterday. What are your thoughts on how we should start our searches?"

JD answered, "Let's go photo by photo and categorize each object by type, then any specific characteristics, such as inscriptions or markings."

Joy agreed, "I'll develop a spreadsheet to record the information. Just tell me the type of object that's in the photograph, then any the inscription or distinctive marking or etching that may be on it."

Joy quickly developed a data record, "Okay, guys! Let's get started."

Daniel looked at a photo, "Item 1 is a gold cross that stands on a dark walnut base. There's an inscription that says, 'White Hall Presbyterian Church, 1839."

"Got it! Next!"

JD described the next item, "Item 2 is a silver plate with the inscription, "To Father Simpson, for your service to St. Benedict's Parish."

"Sounds it may have come from a Roman Catholic Church," mused Joy as she entered the data.

Over the next two hours, Daniel and JD took turns describing each artifact to Joy. After completing the last entry, Joy said, "Looks like we have a good start. What's next?"

JD spoke up, "Let's do some on-line browsing to see if we can find more information on each item. Each of us can take a category—minister's name, church name, or geographical location—and search for additional information."

"I'll take the minister's names!" volunteered Joy.

JD opted, "I'll take the church names."

"That makes it simple," grinned Daniel. "I'll do the geographical locations and compare the maps of the 1860s with current maps. Let's find as much as we can, then we'll compile our information and get it ready to report to the rest of the folks."

Chapter Twenty-Three

Stephen and Tim drove to the Vienna subway station and rode the rail to the National Archives. Once they arrived at the Archives, Stephen helped Tim get a researcher's card, then went to the fourth floor. Stephen was glad they were able to find two side-by-side microfilm readers not in use.

They laid their backpacks on a table, then went to the file cabinets to search for the service and pension records of Lieutenant Lucius Purdy. They found two sets of reels and went back to their microfilm work stations. Stephen agreed to look at Lieutenant Purdy's service record index while Tim looked for his pension record index information. After spinning their reels, they located Purdy's records, but there was something unusual with both sets. For some reason, there were two Lieutenant Purdy's from the same army unit. Stephen and Tim filled out request slips to see both sets of service and pension records.

Thirty minutes later, they went down to the circulation desk on the second floor to pick up their envelopes. Looking through the files, both men were very surprised at what they found.

After making copies and handing the document envelopes back to the librarian, Tim looked at Stephen, "I think we have enough time to look for the service records of Sergeant Benjamin Carmichael and Corporal Amos Devereaux. What do you think?"

"Let's do it!"

They went back to the fourth floor and found the index reels for the service records of Sergeant Benjamin Carmichael and Corporal Amos Devereaux. They repeated the process of requesting both sets of files and obtaining the large, brown envelopes of records. Tim looked at Sergeant Carmichael's service record, and Stephen reviewed Corporal Devereaux's. They were amazed at what they read.

"I think this clears up quite a bit of the mystery," said Tim.

"It sure surprised me!" chuckled Stephen.

They photocopied both sets of records, then returned the records back to the librarian. It was all they could do to remain quiet until they exited the Archives. Once outside, their nonstop conversation continued until they got back to Loft Mountain.

Chapter Twenty-Four

"Lisa, do you still have on-line access to the family research website?" asked Cassie.

"Yes, I do. What are you thinking about?" asked Lisa.

"Let's see if we can find out what happened with Sergeant Willis. I wonder if he died after being so severely wounded."

"Okay! Let's see what we can find on him."

Lisa and Cassie searched the internet for several minutes for anything pertaining to Sergeant Samuel Willis. All they found was that he was declared missing in action after October 1864. They sat back in their chairs and started to shoot ideas off of one another.

"What if he stayed in Virginia after the war?" queried Cassie. "We can't seem to find him anywhere in New York."

"It's worth a try," replied Lisa.

Lisa entered the search query to locate the 1870 Virginia census records. When it came up, she entered the search request for Samuel Willis. Cassie mouthed, "Oh, my word!" when she saw the search results. It listed a Reverend Samuel Willis of the First Methodist Church in Elkton, Virginia.

As they read through the results, they discovered that the church was still in existence. Cassie said, "Stephen and Tim will be driving by Elkton on their way home. I'm going to call them and have them take a detour to see if they can find any more information about Samuel Willis."

She tapped her cell, "Stephen, would you and Tim mind stopping by the First Methodist Church in Elkton?"

"Why?"

"Because according to the 1870 Virginia census records, that's where a Reverend Samuel Willis was minister!"

"Wow! You're kidding! Hey, Tim, guess what Cassie and Lisa found!"

Chapter Twenty-Five

The following morning, everyone returned to the ranger station ready to share what they had found the previous day. As Daniel stood before the group, they heard a knock at the station door. Matt opened the door, then stepped back—it was the Chief Park Ranger with two other rangers.

Chief spoke, "We were given an invitation to come from Joy Nighthawk. She guaranteed we would be surprised by the results of the research y'all have done concerning the soldier's remains."

Everyone introduced themselves to their visitors and invited them to be seated.

Daniel resumed speaking, " Unfortunately, with any items that were melted into ingots, there's no way of knowing what the artifacts were nor who owned them. However, Joy, JD, and I have examined photographs of the remaining gold and silver artifacts and found inscriptions identifying several 1865-era churches.

Using the names of churches and ministers found on the artifacts, JD and Joy searched the internet and located churches and religious-based organizations within a 25-mile radius of our current location that existed during the Civil War.

We correlated that information to present-day maps of the area and discovered many of these churches and religious orders are still in existence today. As a result, we are confident that we were able to identify at least 15 churches and 4 religious organizations as the original owners of the artifacts we found.

Our recommendation is that the Park Service return the gold and silver artifacts to the original churches and organizations. However, we're not sure what to do with the ingots of gold and silver."

Turning to the Chief Park Ranger, Daniel stated, "That's where we're trusting the best judgment of Park Service. Here's a copy of our report." He handed the Chief a thumb drive, then took his seat.

The Chief Park Ranger nodded his head, "We'll take your recommendations into consideration. I'd like to hear what else y'all have found."

Cassie and Lisa stood to give their presentation. Lisa began, "We looked up Sergeant Samuel Willis in the Civil War records on line. We were able to confirm that he was wounded badly in October 1864. He was found almost dead by Confederate Partisan Rangers led by Captain Randolph. The Partisans took him to their captain's home in Rockingham County, Virginia. The captain's family tended to his wounds and nursed him for many weeks until he recovered. During his time of recovery, Samuel tried to find out what had happened to Lundy, but to no avail.

Also during his recovery, Samuel discovered a package addressed to Mary Doherty inside his saddlebag. He asked Captain Randolph to mail the package to Lundy's wife in Michigan. After the war ended, Samuel tried unsuccessfully to contact Lundy's wife by mail and by telegraph. He did not know that after the war, she had moved with her son to the Indian Territory."

Cassie continued with the story, "It appears that Samuel Willis married the Partisan captain's sister. She would read to him each day from the Bible. The more he heard, the more Sergeant Samuel Willis became convinced that he should become a minister of the Gospel. He became a popular speaker throughout the Shenandoah Valley, with a strong passion for preaching.

He would often use the text from John 15:13 as the theme for many of his sermons: 'Greater love hath no man than this, that a man lay down his life for his friends.'

Lisa and I found out that Samuel Willis was the minister at the First Methodist Church in Elkton, Virginia. Yesterday Stephen went by the church to see if they had any additional information concerning Samuel Willis. Stephen, will you share with us what you've found?"

Lisa and Cassie sat down as Stephen got up from his chair, taking several documents with him to the front of the room. "Tim and I drove to the church in Elkton. We were fortunate to meet with Reverend Richard Sheppard.

When we asked him if there were any records on Reverend Samuel Willis, he became very excited and asked us to follow him down a particular hallway. In the hallway were several paintings—one of them was of Reverend Samuel Willis. Tim is passing out copies of the painting. As you can see, he is quite distinguished looking.

After Reverend Sheppard showed us the painting, he told us about a special folder he had found one day as he was cleaning out old files. It had belonged to Reverend Willis and contained several documents, including an account written by Private Doherty. Tim would you mind reading it?"

Tim began, "Over the next several weeks, we were stationed in the Shenandoah Valley in Virginia. I was often given the assignment to work in the telegraph office to code messages from the general officers to be transmitted over the telegraph line and to decipher incoming messages from Washington, D.C.

One evening, after I had finished coding a message for transmission, I was relieved of duty to return to camp. As I walked out of the telegraph office, I heard two voices speaking in low, secretive tones. One of the voices seemed familiar and authoritative. This voice boasted to the other person about all the gold, silver, and jewels they had taken from the Roman Catholic chapel and the Sisters of Faith Convent a few miles north of town. He also recounted how they had burned the paintings and broken the heads off the religious statues inside the chapel. They both snickered when he told about how one of the men had tried, but could not, wrestle a gold ring off of the finger of one of the Sisters of Faith.

The more I heard, the angrier I became. Then I heard the one with the authoritative voice tell the other person to inform the men about a raid planned the following afternoon on the Episcopal Church five miles due south. After the raid, everyone would meet at their rendezvous point to prepare a shipment of gold, silver, and jewels for transport up north.

I waited in the shadows for some time until I could not hear the voices anymore. I looked around the corner of the building and saw the two men walking away from each other. In the bright moonlight, I could make out the familiar figure of Lieutenant Lucius Purdy of the Corps of Engineers. He and his men were often detailed with the Signal Corps whenever new telegraph lines needed to be installed.

Immediately, I reported what I had heard to Sergeant Willis. He told me that we needed to see Captain Goode as soon as possible. After reporting what I had overheard, Captain Goode gave Sergeant Willis and me orders to follow Lieutenant Purdy the following afternoon and report back to him what transpired. He warned us that this would be dangerous and not to say a word to anyone else. We saluted him and replied that we understood the danger.

At the break of dawn, Sergeant Willis woke me up and said that there must have been a change of plans because Lieutenant

Purdy and his men had ridden out of camp during the night.

The sergeant and I quickly mounted our horses and rode south to the old Episcopal Church. However, by the time we got there, it was too late—the church was already burning. Then we spotted an old man dressed in clerical garments laying nearby on the ground. I grabbed a canteen from my horse and went to where the badly wounded man was being propped up by Sergeant Willis.

After taking a few sputtering sips of water, he was able to tell us that he was Reverend Niemeyer. He said that early in the morning, a Union Army lieutenant and his men had broken into his living quarters in the church and demanded to know where he kept all the gold and silver. Reverend Niemeyer told them that the only gold and silver they had were the chalices and crosses used in worship and that he would not give over those sacred items.

The lieutenant became angry and ordered his men to take the Reverend outside. There the lieutenant beat Reverend Niemeyer, shouting and demanding to know where he had hidden the gold and silver. Again, Reverend Niemeyer told him that these were sacred items used in worshipping and honoring Christ our Savior. The lieutenant gave orders to his men to strike him with their rifle butts. They continued striking him again and again until he fell to the ground. Again, lieutenant demanded to know the location of the gold and silver. Again, the Reverend kept quiet. Then the lieutenant ordered his men to fix bayonets on their rifles, then they followed his next order to use Reverend Niemeyer for bayonet practice. They continued until he passed out, falling to the ground where the Sergeant and I found him.

We started washing and dressing Reverend Niemeyer's wounds. Within a few moments, we heard horses coming, and we hoped it was a Union patrol that would help us.

As the horsemen came into view, we saw that it was a patrol of Confederate Partisan Rangers. Sergeant Willis and I were quickly surrounded by about a dozen men on cavalry mounts. The officer in charge of the patrol dismounted and told us that we were now prisoners of the Confederate army.

As I raised my right hand, the leader saw the ring on my finger and asked if I was a Mason. I replied that I was indeed a Mason. He ordered his men to lower their rifles. Then he took off his gauntlet and showed me his own Masonic ring.

Once the rifles were lowered, Sergeant Willis told him about what had happened to Reverend Niemeyer and how we had found him. The officer of the patrol introduced himself as Captain Randolph and ordered his men to help us tend to Reverend Niemeyer.

As we worked, Reverend Niemeyer repeated his story for Captain Randolph. As he spoke, he became weaker and weaker. Eventually, his breathing slowed to a minimum, then Reverend Niemeyer took his last breath and passed on to eternity.

Together we all buried Reverend Niemeyer in the cemetery next to the burned-out church. Afterward, the captain thanked us for showing mercy and compassion toward Reverend Niemeyer. Sergeant Willis told him that it was our Christian responsibility.

We assured the captain that we were heading back to our camp to report the atrocity and to have the lieutenant and his men arrested and tried for their crimes. Captain Randolph gave us a pass allowing us safe passage through the area in case there were other Confederate patrols. After thanking him, we mounted our horses and started toward the wooded area where we thought Lieutenant Purdy and his men had gone."

Tim said, "That's all he wrote in this report. But the folder also included an account written by Reverend Samuel Willis, formerly Sergeant Samuel Willis, U.S. Signal Corps. Stephen, care to do the honors?"

Stephen stood up, document in hand. "Lundy and I dismounted near a hemlock hollow a few miles east of Port Republic when we saw smoke coming from inside a cave. We heard voices and quietly stepped closer to the cave where we overheard a plan to steal more gold and to melt down the items they already had stolen. We went back to our horses, and Lundy started to do some code writing.

Suddenly, rifle fire started cracking around us. We went for our weapons, but I was grazed on the head by a minié ball, then took a bullet in the shoulder. Doherty would not let me fall. He rushed me to my horse, got me on it, and told me to ride back to camp. He said he would cover my retreat. I didn't want to leave him, but Doherty slapped the rump of my horse before I could dismount.

As I rode away, I heard more shots, but it wasn't long before I couldn't hear them anymore. Everything in my head seemed to whirl about for quite some time. I know I must have traveled quite a ways, but I simply don't remember much of what happened after that. However, there is one thing of which I am very certain—my friend, Lundy Doherty, gave his life so that I could live."

After a quiet moment, Tim spoke again, "As you know, Stephen and I went to the National Archives yesterday. There we searched for the service records of Lieutenant Lucius Purdy, Sergeant Benjamin Carmichael, and Corporal Amos Devereaux - the ones who wrote the letters condemning Private Doherty and Sergeant Willis as traitors.

We were surprised to find that there were actually two Lieutenant Lucius Purdys in the Union Army. The first Lieutenant Lucius Purdy came from Ohio and was killed in the battle of Fredericksburg, Virginia. The second Lucius Purdy was really Corporal Michael Bean of Pittsburgh, Pennsylvania.

He was there at Fredericksburg as an enlisted man in a Pennsylvania infantry regiment when the real Lieutenant Purdy was killed by enemy. Bean and a detail of men were assigned to bury the dead after the battle. When they came to Lieutenant Purdy, Bean stripped the jacket and uniform from the body and assumed the identity of the Lieutenant. The men who were with him on burial detail became a part of his "command".

It seems that this fraudulent Lieutenant Purdy and his men reported to the U.S. Signal Corps after the battle and became attached to that command. It's amazing that no one seemed to question his identity. This second "Lieutenant Purdy" is the one who had given a negative report about Sergeant Willis and Private Doherty."

Stephen picked up the story next, "After giving that report to his commanding officer, Lieutenant Purdy (aka Bean) and his men received orders to report that same day to Winchester to support another group of engineers in restoring telegraph lines leading to Washington, D.C. and in rebuilding bridges across the Shenandoah River. Little did they realize that a few days later on October 19, 1864, they would get caught up in a battle known as Cedar Creek, Virginia. They were captured and sent to a prison in Danville, Virginia.

Shortly afterwards, Bean was sent to Libby Prison in Richmond, Virginia, and slowly died of complications from scurvy and diarrhea. Carmichael and Devereaux were eventually transferred to Andersonville Prison in Georgia. Within a few weeks after arriving there, both died of disease and starvation. We don't know what happened to the other men in Bean's command."

Quiet pervaded the room as everyone took the time to reflect on what had been shared. Eventually, they turned to look at each other. The Chief Park Ranger spoke, "Joy was right–this definitely was worth the trip. Y'all have done excellent work. I can promise you that the National Park Service will help in any way it can to finish the work you've started." After promising to keep in touch, the Chief and other rangers left the station.

Cassie turned to the group, "We need to pray about what to do next. We need God's help. Tim, would you lead us in prayer?"

The group gathered in a circle and joined hands. All heads were bowed and eyes were closed in reverence. Tim began, "Father, we stand here amazed at the truth that has lain dormant for so long. We know that the Savior whom Sergeant Samuel Willis and Private Edward Lundawick Doherty discovered for themselves during the great American Civil War many, many years ago is the same One who has been working through us over the past several days. We acknowledge You as Lord and Savior! Please provide the guidance we need on how to proceed next. Thank you for allowing us the privilege to try to set things right and bring honor to You! In Jesus' Name, we pray! Amen!"

Chapter Twenty-Six

After the meeting, Lisa and Cassie contacted Jim Doherty in Ramona, Oklahoma, and shared all that had been discovered about his great grandfather. He expressed his deep appreciation and promised to keep in touch.

The group decided it was time to pack up and head back to their respective homes. Saying goodbye to Matt, they thanked him for generously allowing them to use his ranger station during their stay.

Before they broke camp, they had lunch together, sharing observations about their camping adventure. They determined what tasks still needed to be done and made plans to get together again in the near future.

In the weeks that followed, arrangements were made between the Commonwealth of Virginia and the State of Oklahoma to transfer the remains of Private Edward Lundawick Doherty to the capitol building in Oklahoma City, Oklahoma, to lie in state with a military honor guard for three days. Afterward, his remains would be taken to Jim Doherty's family church in Ramona, Oklahoma. Jim invited Stephen and Cassie, Tim and Lisa, Joy, JD, Matt, and Daniel to be his honored guests at Lundy's memorial service. They said they would be honored to attend and would bring with them the daguerreotype of Mary plus Lundy's Masonic ring for Jim Doherty.

The day of the church service was beautiful, and a warm

breeze gently blew around the small crowd at the cemetery. When Jim Doherty's pastor had heard the complete story of Private Edward Lundawick Doherty, he decided that it was appropriate to use the same text that Private Doherty's friend, Sergeant Samuel Willis, had often used when he became a pastor: "Greater love hath no man than this, that he lay down his life for his friends."

When the pastor finished speaking, the military honor guard stood around Lundy's flag-draped casket and honored his memory with a volley of three shots into the air. They finished and stood at attention as an army bugler sounded the stirring, mournful notes of Taps. Then with steady, military precision, the honor guard folded the United States flag that had draped Lundy's casket, and a sergeant handed it to Jim Doherty.

For the family and honored guests, there was a sense of completeness once the memorial service was concluded and Private Edward L. Doherty was laid to rest beside his wife, Mary, after being apart from her for more than 150 years.

Jim Doherty invited the group to his home afterward, and they presented him with Lundy's ring and the daguerreotype of Mary. Jim immediately retrieved the one he had of Edward Lundawick Doherty and hooked both daguerreotypes together, placing them on top of his fireplace mantle. Jim whispered, "Together again–finally."

Epilogue

In Washington D.C., a Federal order was given to correct the service and pension records of Private Doherty to show that he had died honorably in the line of duty and that the documents accusing him of being a traitor be expunged from his records.

Matt Shelbourne contacted the National Park Service concerning the gold and silver artifacts that were found inside the cave near Ivy Creek Spring. After a short period of deliberation, the National Park Service had agreed that the engraved artifacts should be returned to the original churches and religious organizations.

However, an interesting thing happened when all the church leaders and representatives from the region gathered together. They heard the story about Private Doherty and Sergeant Willis and unanimously agreed to use the recovered gold, silver, and jewels to establish a non-profit foundation known as "No Greater Love".

The gold, silver, and jewels would be sold and the funds from the sale would purchase building supplies and materials needed to modify the homes of returning veterans who had been disabled in recent conflicts.

As a way of saying 'thank you', several of the veterans worked together to design and make a display case at the Loft Mountain ranger station for the artifacts found in that hemlock hollow. Many of the veterans also volunteered at the station to recount Doherty's story to the public.

Matt Shelbourne increased the Park's activities by adding a hike to the Ivy Creek hemlock hollow where the remains of Private Doherty were found. At the end of each presentation, Ranger Shelbourne would end with a paraphrase of Lincoln's Gettysburg Address: "The world will little note nor long remember what we say here, but it can never forget what he did here."

After the group's trip to Oklahoma, Daniel was contacted by a major Virginia university and hired to help develop research techniques in anthropological forensics. He also received many requests from universities throughout the country to share the story of how the identity of Private Doherty was determined.

JD completed his PhD work in English Literature. He became quite adept at storytelling and was often invited to be a guest speaker at many colleges and universities, but his favorite venue was to tell stories at Irish festivals throughout the country. The most requested story seemed to be about the Irish American soldier who gave his life so another man could live.

Joy expanded her work in computer forensic technologies by refining holographic imaging to include animation. When Daniel read about her work, he requested the university to hire her as one of the lead researchers in computer forensic technologies. Often she would receive the toughest forensic mysteries to solve. Whenever other researchers would tell her to give up, she would stop what she was doing and share with them the story of solving the identity of Private Edward Doherty.

As for Stephen and Cassie, they planned another camping trip with Tim and Lisa in Southwest Virginia. That fall, the four traveled down the color-laden Blue Ridge Parkway in Floyd County, stopping at Mabry's Mill to listen to area musicians playing bluegrass music and to sample some freshly made apple butter. There was something about the sweet, spicy smell of the apple butter cooking in the copper kettles and the warmth of the wood fires that seemed to draw everyone into the Blue Ridge mountain heritage.

As dusk began to settle that evening, the four friends listened to an older mountain man with a long, grey beard tell a story about his grandfather being an herbal doctor in Floyd County. What intrigued them most was his story of how he played with small brass cannons and small cannon balls when he was a little boy. He used to hide the cannons in a small cave after he had played with them on the old family farm in Floyd County. As he grew older, he forgot their whereabouts. On several occasions, he tried to find them again, but was unsuccessful. The old man sighed, shook his head and concluded his story by saying that he hadn't seen them for over 70 years.

Tim, Lisa, Stephen, and Cassie looked at each other and grinned. Lisa spoke for all of them, "Let's see if we can help you find a different ending to your story!"

Acknowledgements

Since the early stages of writing *Sacrifice at Shenandoah*, my wife has supported this project by listening, critiquing, and editing. Over the years, we've learned that whatever challenges come our way, we can always trust God to be with us. Of our many blessings, the most important are our two children, Joshua and Rebekah, who inspire me with their intelligence and wit.

Tom and Beth Godfrey, the inspiration for Tim and Lisa, have been our friends and pinochle partners for almost 30 years. Their help in editing and critiquing my manuscript is greatly appreciated.

During this project, I asked several of my colleagues from the Professional Grounds Management Society for suggestions to improve the story. Joe Jackson, John Van Etten, Marion Bolick, John Burns, Gerald Landby, and Walt Bonvell - thank you for your valuable input.

For their support and encouragement throughout this project, my thanks go to my Dad; Sandy Eskew; my sisters, Judy and Randi; Ed Allen; and many of the staff members at Cordova Recreation and Park District.

Finally, many thanks to my brother, Kerwin, for believing in the project and helping me get *Sacrifice at Shenandoah* published.

Gerald S. Dobbs